CRYPT OF BONE

AN ARKANE THRILLER
J.F. PENN

Crypt of Bone. An ARKANE Thriller (Book 2)
Copyright © Joanna Penn (2011, 2013, 2015). All rights reserved.
Second Edition. Previously published as PROPHECY

www.JFPenn.com

ISBN: 978-1-912105-72-4

Requests to publish work from this book should be sent to:
joanna@CurlUpPress.com

Cover and Interior Design: JD Smith Design

Printed by Lightning Source

www.CurlUpPress.com

"Before me was a pale horse. Its rider was named Death, and Hades was following close behind him. They were given power over a fourth of the earth to kill by sword, famine and plague, and by the wild beasts of the earth."

Revelation 6:8

DAY 1

PROLOGUE

Jerusalem. Israel. 5.27am

BLOOD HAS SEEPED INTO the stones of Jerusalem for millennia. Screams of the dying have echoed across the Kidron Valley as the ancient city has been besieged, broken and destroyed. Each time, the blood of the defeated has watered the earth, seeds of hate to be harvested in the next generation. Demons of war and power have squatted over the city, feeding off the lives that ground themselves to dust for their gods. Here the blood of human sacrifice stained the altars to Baal and fortress walls were built on the crushed bodies of the vanquished. Here the Jews fought to rule their Holy City, being both victor and then victim in their long history. Here the blood of Jesus Christ ran onto the stone streets of the Old City as the mob jeered his passing. Jerusalem has always been a place of blood, and always will be.

Ayal Ben-David stepped out from the maze of Jewish Quarter streets onto the series of ramps leading down to the Western Wall. The golden Dome of the Rock dominated the scene, reflecting the rays of the rising sun. The blue tiles were dusky from this distance but Ayal knew the mosque was covered with Arabic script and brilliant turquoise, aqua and gold tiles. It stood framed by cypress trees, witnesses to a never-ending conflict. Ayal walked across the wide expanse of the open square, grey marble reflecting pink hues of the early morning sky. He raised his hand to another soldier standing guard at the eastern entrance to the square, acknowledging him but not stopping.

Ayal stood taller as he neared the Western Wall itself, straightening his uniform and checking that his rifle hung down correctly behind him. He never tired of this morning routine. This wall was the only remnant of the ancient Temple and Jews had been kept from it for so long. It was the closest they could get to the Temple Mount where God gathered the dust to fashion Adam, where Abraham had bound his son Isaac as a sacrifice. It had been the centre of the Jewish temple, the Holy of Holies, the place where God dwelt with His chosen people. But it was also here that Mohammad ascended to heaven on his Night Journey and so it had become the most contested religious site in the world.

Ayal was close enough now to see the huge blocks of limestone that made up the ancient wall. Each was almost as tall as a man, the wall's foundations embedded deep in the earth. There were tufts of shikaron or henbane spiking from the grooves between the blocks. Ayal smiled as a swallow swooped to perch and pick an insect from one of the thorny bushes that grew there. Nature found its way into the cracks of life, he thought, like the Jews, surviving despite genera-tions of persecution. Ayal was proud. This was his heritage, his life.

He stood in front of the wall and began to pray, finger-tips resting gently against the stone. He could almost feel the power of the place. Hopes and prayers of believers were written on scraps of paper and pushed into the cracks of stone. The tefillah, heartfelt prayers, would reach God faster here, the most holy place, where the real bled into the divine. As he neared the end of the first prayer, Ayal heard shouting above him. The words were muffled but the noise echoed through the square. Immediately, he swung his rifle into position, looking up for potential danger. Rocks had been thrown down many times by Muslims intent on disrupting the prayers of the Jewish faithful, but sometimes the threat was more serious. He could see that the other soldiers in position around the square had heard the noise and were also prepared for action. Moving back away from the wall, Ayal scanned for the source of the noise.

Standing on top of the Western Wall, a skinny man in a thin white robe raised his hands to the dawn sky and called out to God. His head was shaved and his skeletal figure made a grotesque outline against the deepening azure sky. Ayal couldn't make out the words but clearly the man was a fanatic and the guards from the Temple Mount would get to him soon enough. Ayal turned his head to signal to the others to stand down; there was no real threat. But a soldier was pointing urgently, and Ayal looked back to see the man jump from the top of the wall, sixty feet above him. The man was silent as he fell, white robe billowing behind him in a parody of flight. With a sickening crunch, his body smashed on the flagstones at the base of the wall. Blood exploded from the broken body, staining the robe into a grisly shroud.

Ayal ran to the man, but he could see there was nothing to be done, for he was clearly already dead. He knelt and checked the man's pulse out of protocol, then called for another soldier to bring screens to put around the body. He would need the Rabbi to come and cleanse the area before the worshippers arrived. Ayal noticed that the man was young, maybe in his thirties. Although half of his face was mangled by the fall, he had sharply defined cheekbones, as though he had been starving. Strangely, his face wasn't contorted and it seemed he had died at peace. There were no other wounds so he hadn't been shot. He had just jumped.

Ayal could see that the once white gown was from a hospital and that the man was naked underneath. He moved the gown slightly to cover the man and give him some dignity in death. As he bent down, Ayal noticed a scrap of paper that had been clutched in the man's hand and now lay crumpled next to the body. Perhaps it would give some clue as to why he jumped. Blood was still oozing from the body and would soak the scrap before long so he picked it up. It showed a roughly drawn horse's head in thick lines of charcoal, smudged into the page with rough hands. The horse's eyes were wide, its nostrils flared. Chalk had been rubbed over it to give a consistent white appearance. Beneath the image were inked the words, 'Before me was a pale horse. Its rider was named Death, and Hades followed close behind.' Ayal recognized it as part of a Christian prophecy from the book of Revelation and for a moment he pondered its significance.

As he stood to direct the other soldiers, a trickle of blood ran down into the cracks of stone beneath his feet, joining the blood that had soaked the earth of the holy city for millennia.

CHAPTER 1

Oxford, England. 6.43am

THE VERDANT GREEN OF summer was intensified by the rain that pounded down. It darkened the day, shadowing the earth in cloud. Morgan Sierra ran through the gates of the University Parks by Keble College, her stride lengthening as she headed towards the river Cherwell. In the distance she could hear the rumbling of thunder as it grew closer and lightning forked towards her from the north. This was Morgan's favorite time to run. When most people hurried inside, she quickly changed into her gear and sprinted towards the storm. She had always been a chaser of violent weather. It thrilled her to move over the earth connected to this power of Nature, yet it was rare to have such tropical storms in England. This was a country of gentle rolling hills and soft rain that pattered onto the leaves of spreading oak trees. English rain was persistent but rarely violent so this was an event to be savored.

The rain made the ground slippery and Morgan was soaked through, t-shirt slick against her skin. She was more a thing of water than of air, her breathing even and pace strong as she raced through the park. She came out at St Catherine's College, crossed the river and continued towards Magdalen Bridge. Oak trees shaded the path, a canopy of mottled jade, leaves open to the rain. Morgan splashed through puddles, a smile growing wider on her face. Sprinting now, she pushed herself as hard as she could along the towpath until she finally reached the crossing point at Magdalen. Panting, she stopped to catch her breath, skin cooling in the downpour. I needed this, she thought. I need to push myself physically to feel alive. A nagging part of her knew that her attraction to ARKANE lay in this acknowledged truth. She had felt alive during the search for the Pentecost stones and then the Arcane Religious Knowledge And Numinous Experience Institute had offered her a job. That had been almost a month ago and still she couldn't decide her response.

Morgan ran on through the Botanical Gardens towards the junction where the Cherwell met the Isis, that part of the Thames that belonged to Oxford. Running helped her think, gave her body something to do while she mentally processed. The storm was a bonus, a way to hide and also to clear the paths of Oxford which heaved with tourists in the summer months. Morgan had thought about resurrecting her clinical psychology practice, but the problems of individual patients no longer seemed as challenging as the mysteries that ARKANE agents were investigating. She was distracted and it showed in her patient numbers. The University was quiet over the summer months, when she was meant to be writing scientific papers and improving her academic standing. But the work seemed insignificant in the face of almost losing her sister and niece. At the thought of little Gemma, Morgan ran harder, her love and fear needing the outlet. She would do it all again to keep them safe.

Then there were the memories of the firefight in her office. ARKANE had done a great job of clearing up the bodies and repairing her furniture, but her Jungian mandala was forever stained with dark blood and her bookcases pock-marked with bullet-holes. Morgan knew that she should be more affected by the deaths, by her own ability to kill. It was self-defense, but she had felt the thrill of battle again. Some people just didn't get post traumatic stress; she knew that academically as a psychologist. Those types of people made excellent soldiers, accomplished assassins. Perhaps not brilliant academics. She thought of her father then. He too had loved the rain and the storms. Living in Israel, rain had been so precious. Through the back-breaking work of Jewish immigrants, they had made the desert bloom, the kibbutzim a family of life-bringers. Her father would have been so proud of her place at Oxford, but then he had also been desperately proud of her place in the Israeli Defense Force. She smiled. He would have approved of a warrior academic.

Morgan emerged onto the Isis river bank at the end of Christchurch meadow as the storm broke over her head. Lightning cracked the sky and thunder rolled past immediately. Cattle in the meadow huddled together under the trees, heads down. Local swans floated in loving pairs on the river, splattered by huge drops of rain. Ripples overlapped each other, spreading out to slap against the side of canal boats tethered on the banks, their bright shutters closed against the deluge. Morgan ran up the wide pathway towards Christchurch College, the power in the storm transferred to her through the crackling air. She recognized that the energy she felt now, the exhilaration, was what she had felt working with ARKANE and with Jake Timber.

Catching her breath again, Morgan set off at an easier pace towards the imposing college and again considered her options. Going back to the practice in the last few weeks had felt more like an end than a new beginning. Working with ARKANE would give her the chance she needed to develop her skills further and it would give her access to their unique and diverse material. Morgan smiled to herself, and thought, let's face it, clinical practice just isn't as exciting as exploring the spiritual mysteries of the world.

She had spent nights dreaming of the underground vault that ARKANE kept hidden under London's Trafalgar Square. There were mysteries locked away down there, a kaleidoscope of mankind's spiritual history. She had a chance to be part of that world. She only had to pick up the phone to call Director Marietti. But part of her still stung from the betrayal and the secrets they had kept from her, the fight she had with Jake. Yet he still haunted her dreams as well. Sometimes she woke from a vivid dream of them together, physical violence morphing into passionate sex. She hadn't heard from him since she had walked away from the ARKANE vault. Perhaps he never thought of her at all.

The storm was retreating now, thunder taking longer between the lightning strikes. Even the rain was easing to a gentler refrain. Now that the frenzy of the storm had passed, the city was washed and shone in the morning sun. Morgan jogged towards Walton Street, her pace slowing. She had always dreamed of working at Oxford. Now she was a respected academic at this great University, with her own private clinical practice. She was close to her family. How could it be any better than this? So why did she feel so conflicted?

CHAPTER 2

Ezra Institute. Jerusalem, Israel. 8.32am

THE EZRA INSTITUTE WAS in chaos. Somehow one of the patients had escaped and they were still searching for him. The alarm had gone off before dawn and the bell still rang at intervals, jolting everyone anew. A team had been sent out with the police to try to find him, so the Institute was short-staffed. But something else had triggered a reaction in the patients and Dinah Mizrahi had been called in to sort it out. As Deputy Director of the facility, she was frequently left to deal with emergencies while her boss spent his time dealing with fundraising. At least that's what he called it, Dinah thought as she hurried down the tiled corridor. There was a problem in the women's ward. She could hear the wailing all the way to the reception area. At the door to the ward, the security guard asked for her pass.

"Seriously, Mikael. Do we have to go through this every morning?" She fumbled at her waist for the card.

"You know the rules, Dr Mizrahi," the guard said with a smile, used to the routine. He knew that the complaining medical staff were truly grateful for the protection in this dangerous city. He buzzed her into the main facility.

Only Israel could possibly have a place like Ezra, a specialized institution for those suffering from Jerusalem

Syndrome. It manifested as a set of mental phenomena associated with the religious aspects of the Holy City, generally affecting Christians and some Jews. Patients thought they were Mary, the mother of Christ, or John the Baptist, Elijah or other religious figures connected with Jerusalem. They often claimed to be messengers from God. Many recovered when they were removed from the city but some were too entrenched in their psychoses and they were brought here to Ezra. The women's ward had four Mary, mother of Jesus and three Mary Magdalenes. Today they were united in a chorus of wailing, an intense outpouring of grief.

Entering the ward, Dinah saw Abigail, the ward Sister, struggling to cope with the mass emotion in the usually well behaved ward.

"Do you know what triggered this?" Dinah shouted, struggling to be heard above the din.

"It started suddenly, just after dawn," Abigail replied. "They won't speak. They just wail. They're inconsolable. I didn't want to sedate them until you'd seen them like this."

"Thank you but I think we can sedate them now. The other patients will be fretting with the noise. Have there been any other incidents?"

The nurse looked at the floor.

"I'm so sorry Dr Mizrahi but the Marys have taken all my attention. We're short staffed at the best of times. I haven't even had time to check on the others."

Dinah dismissed the nurse's concern.

"It's alright, I'll go check on them now. I'll start with Abraham."

Dinah headed down the long corridor towards the wing where patients were kept in individual rooms. It wasn't solitary confinement so much as a private mini ward where the patients couldn't hurt others. They had tried bigger wards but the re-enactment of certain biblical events had caused them to keep the more seriously affected separate. The patient called Abraham had been there almost two months now. He had never given them another name and had no ID on him when he had been admitted. He was clearly well versed in scripture and Dinah couldn't fault his knowledge. With her combined expertise in psychiatry and theology, she felt Abraham was one of the patients most deeply embedded in his own psychoses. He truly believed that he was Abraham, the prophet of God, servant of the Most High. The only patient who came close to this was Daniel, who had escaped from the facility this morning. He believed himself to be John of Patmos, the writer of Revelation. Dinah decided to visit Abraham first and then check Daniel's room to see if there were any clues to his disappearance.

The corridor she walked down was bright basic white with no decorations. The Institute team had found that any kind of visual stimulation was interpreted by the patients as a message from God. As she approached Abraham's door, she could hear a low voice praying in a stream of connected words. At least he wasn't screaming the place down, Dinah thought. Then she looked through the glass window into the small room, and immediately pressed the alarm call button next to the door.

Dinah swiped her card and burst into the room. The stench of blood and feces made her flinch and she put a hand to her nose as she took in the scene. Abraham was kneeling on the floor by the bed, his eyes glazed and staring. He was naked, rocking his body back and forth as he prayed on his knees in a pool of blood. At the end of each string of prayers, he cut himself with a long razor blade, eyes unflinching. In some places it looked as if he had sliced down to the bone. He hadn't hit a major artery yet but his blood already soaked the floor. Dinah crouched near him, down on his level but out of the reach of the razor. Protocol said she shouldn't even be in there, she should wait for security, but she knew this man. She could help him. If he didn't stop soon he would bleed to death.

"Abraham, can you hear me?" she said in a low calm voice.

He continued praying but in a louder tone as if to drown her out. Dinah couldn't make out his words. She tried again.

"Abraham, you're safe now. Please talk to me."

He seemed to be winding up towards a crescendo in his prayers, and Dinah willed the security guards to get there faster. If they could just sedate him, the cutting would stop.

"It's OK," she said. "Just put down the razor now."

Abraham went silent and cocked his head as if listening. Reversing his grip, he suddenly rose on his knees and plunged the razor blade deep into his belly, grunting as he ripped it across and down. He fell sideways to the floor.

"No ... no!" Dinah shouted and reached for him, unafraid of the blade now as it had served its dark purpose. She crawled through the blood to gather Abraham in her arms. A stream of blood and entrails erupted from his belly, as he had effectively disemboweled himself with the sharp instrument. The noxious smell made her gag but she held him anyway. His eyes flickered open.

"Why Abraham, why?" Dinah pleaded.

For a moment she saw lucidity there. He seemed entirely rational and spoke in barely a whisper.

"God told me to do it. I had to obey."

His breath rasped and then quieted, his last sound a sigh. Dinah felt a part of him slip away as the alarms rang on and the guards finally arrived with the crash cart. But they were too late. Dinah sat there holding Abraham's body, her white coat and hands covered in gore. She looked up to the wall above his bed. Scrawled there in blood and feces was a line drawing, a horse rearing up on its back legs as if to crush the body below. The rider on the horse was a black wraith, as if Death itself had come to claim this victim.

J.F. PENN

"Dr Mizrahi? We need to take the body." One of the orderlies spoke from the door, a new guy funded by the last grant from Zoebios.

"Of course, sorry ... I just thought ... I thought I could get to him in time."

Dinah tried to rise, slipping in the bloody mess. He helped her stand, supporting her to the door.

"Sometimes there's no stopping them," he said. "This one looked on the edge,"

Dinah looked at him more closely, something in his tone alerting her.

"Sorry, I don't remember your name."

"It's Jacobsen, I only started last week. It seemed like a relatively quiet place then, but now this and of course, Daniel."

"What have you heard about Daniel?" Dinah asked with growing concern. "I haven't been able to get to his room yet. Is he still missing?"

The orderly shook his head.

"Word just came in that he's dead too. Jumped from the top of the Western Wall. The Army have his body and they're sending someone to talk to you later." Dinah looked up at the looming figure of Death on the wall. He had claimed two of her patients today and she would not see him take another. Something had changed, something was wrong here. She didn't trust her boss, didn't trust the others here, but there was someone she did trust. It was time to call in a favor from a friend she hadn't seen in far too long.

CHAPTER 3

Oxford, England. 7.38am

MORGAN SAT IN THE window seat of her tiny Jericho house, muscles aching from the run. The alcove had been one of the reasons she had bought the two up, two down terraced house between Ruskin College and the imposing stonework of the Oxford University Press. It was a sun-trap for a tiny part of the day and in the long, drawn out English winters she needed that glimmer of hope. It was a long way from her Tel Aviv apartment with Elian where they had embraced the pulse of the city, spending balmy nights dancing after long days of work researching military psychology. After Elian's death, she had sold the apartment and now had little desire to be in loud places but she still needed the sun.

This house was her retreat from the mad world of academic Oxford and she barricaded herself in with books and journals. She filled her time with exercise and excess work, a formula to forget what she had lost. A soft meow broke into her thoughts and Morgan patted her lap for the cat to jump up. She had started feeding the little stray and over time it had adopted her. Morgan had named her Lakshmi, Hindu goddess of wealth, prosperity, wisdom and courage which seemed like a good omen when she started to work at Oxford University. The little grey tabby rarely came for a cuddle, being as independent as her mistress. But today she seemed determined to collect her rightful portion of love and Morgan was glad of the company.

The storm had cleared and the sun was out, illuminating a cleaner earth after the rain. Morgan stroked Shmi, her hand scratching behind the cat's ears as she drank her thick black coffee, a Mediterranean addiction. The British just didn't know how to make it properly, she thought; they drowned the bitterness in milk. For a moment, it seemed as if she could just rest here, happy and at peace like the cat curled in her lap. But that's just not me, Morgan thought. I want more than this. Peace is only appreciated as a calm between the adventures.

Morgan flipped open her laptop. One of her daily rituals was to check the news in Israel. With the threat of war from different sides each week, she liked to keep an eye on her old home. She also stayed up to date with the latest in psychological research and religious issues. But before she could flick to the Middle East section, one of the scrolling videos caught her eye with an ambitious headline, 'Global mental health achievable by 2020'. It was a piece on the biotech company Zoebios. Morgan recognized the name as an amalgamation of the Greek words 'zoe', meaning eternal life, and 'bios', used more to mean temporal, physical life. She clicked the video and it streamed a press conference with the CEO, Milan Noble. He was a stunning man, exuding charisma even from the tiny screen, more movie star than corporate suit. He stood a head taller than the sea of journalists, with cropped hair and chiseled jaw. His eyes danced with passion as he described his latest project.

"Zoebios has expanded into China, India and sub-Saharan Africa in the last two years. We are now the largest provider of primary health care for family planning, pregnancy and birth in Europe and the United States. Our research into early life development has raised the bar on child care models throughout the world. Through education of women, we are lowering birth rates and improving life expectancy across the globe."

The screen changed to show images of Zoebios facilities with multi-cultural doctors, happy mothers and healthy bouncing babies. As Milan Noble continued, Morgan noticed a trace of Eastern European in his cultured accent.

"But my vision for an improved human race goes far beyond physical health," he said. "Mental health problems are destroying lives, with increasing numbers of people on medication just to get through the day." He paused for dramatic effect. "But there is a way to tackle depression and anxiety without drugs. The trials we have run in multiple countries have been successful and we are now releasing this methodology to the wider public free of charge. You have trusted Zoebios with your children and the results speak for themselves, now trust us with your own health. You can register for information packs at our website. Thank you."

As journalists clamored to ask more questions, the camera faded to show the Zoebios logo, an unfurling shoot of new life, and the company website address. Morgan was intrigued, since depression and anxiety were now the most common mental health issues, causing untold suffering to many and costing millions in healthcare. If Zoebios had a non-invasive, non-drug related treatment, it would be phenomenally successful and she was interested in reading more about their research. She clicked the link to have a look at their site just as her cellphone rang.

"Morgan, it's Di."

Morgan's face broke into a genuine smile at her old friend's voice. Dinah had been her room-mate and best friend in Israel but their busy lives meant they didn't talk as much as they both wanted to. Yet when they spoke it was as if time melted away. The memories they shared made a lifetime bond, and they owed each other much for the times of support and friendship.

"Thank goodness you're there," Dinah continued. "I need your help with something."

"Are you ok? You sound upset, what is it?"

There was a pause as if her friend didn't know how to start.

"It's Ezra. There's something strange going on. We've had two suicides and I can't understand why. There's no one else I trust here, Morgan, and certainly no one with your experience. You know how well we work together. Any chance you can come to Jerusalem?"

Morgan smiled to herself. Be careful what you wish for, she thought.

"It just so happens that I might have a space in my schedule. When do you need me?"

"As soon as you can get here."

"Of course. It might be time for a little trip home anyway. I miss you Di. It's been too long, and we have so much to catch up on. I can get a flight late tonight so I should be with you by breakfast."

"You're a blessing, Morgan. I can't wait to see you. You're going to find this disturbing but fascinating. See you tomorrow."

Morgan hung up the phone and headed to the bedroom to pack, excited at the chance to be involved in a new mystery. She caught sight of the photo on the mantelpiece and paused to pick it up. Her own smiling face looked out, along with her twin sister Faye, and Gemma, her two year old niece. She and Faye both had cobalt blue eyes with a curious slash of violet, Morgan's in the right eye and Faye's in the left. But the physical resemblance ended there and their personalities couldn't have been more different, just like their parents. Born on the cusp of Aquarius and Pisces, Morgan's independence had pushed her into the world first. Their parents' bitter separation meant they had grown up separately but Morgan felt that finally they were getting to know each other. She knew she would do anything for Gemma. The events of Pentecost had threatened all of their lives and Morgan wouldn't risk that again. This next step would be hers alone.

CHAPTER 4

Sedlec Chapel, Kutna Hora, Czech Republic. 11.02pm

FRANCO MESSINA HAD BEEN to Sedlec before, but never in the middle of the night when the bones of the crypt seemed to glow. What was sickly yellow in the day, resonant of pus and decay, was transformed into golden marvel in the candlelight. Incense hung in the air, delicate smoke blurring the edges of the scene. The ossuary contained around fifty thousand skeletons arranged in bony sculptures and macabre shapes. Most of the bones came from the Black Death but there were rumors that other bodies had been hidden here. For who would notice fresh bones in the bell shaped mounds in the shadows of the chapel? Franco looked up at the great chandelier, which apparently contained bones from every part of the human body. It had eight candelabra, each made of a spinal column with vertebrae lining the arms. Femurs hung down, the balls of the knee joint rounded and smooth. Candles were cradled by plates of pelvis bone, each topped with a skull. Everything was nailed into place and that made Franco shiver a little. Bones don't bleed but the nails were an offense, forcing these dead to their display of ashen grace. Ropes of skulls with crossed bones were draped around the vault, empty eye sockets peering down at the gathering crowd below. We are all reduced to this, Franco thought, just another femur, just another skull. He shook his head to clear the depressing thoughts.

Franco stood in front of Ivan, who had brought him here tonight after long months of proving himself worthy of this final privilege. Tonight he would be part of the Thanatos ceremony, the culmination of his trials. Franco knew the rewards this would bring. He saw the riches that Ivan had been putting away and it was what he wanted too. He had been recruited several months ago, when Ivan had seen him fighting in a bar brawl. Perhaps he had taken it a bit far that night, the man's face mashed to a pulp. But after that, Ivan had asked him to do some 'security' work and had encouraged him to invest in his fighting skills. After a few weeks Ivan had introduced him to other men who were part of the Thanatos network. Together they formed a vigilante group, taking out unwanted parts of the community based on directives from above. Some people might call them surgical strikes, cutting out the bad parts of society so that the good could thrive. Franco was a believer in nationalism. He didn't want the gypsies or the rag-heads, the crazies, beggars or fags around. Who did? He didn't even draw the line at women, prostitutes who diluted the family values of the city, but he always had his fun first. It was easy work, paid well and the police seemed to look the other way.

Franco touched his arm where the tattoo would be added after tonight. Ivan had said that he would be eligible for full membership after the ceremony and the tattoo protected those who wore it. If you had the tattoo and were caught, there were always men around who would get you out of trouble. It was currency, valuable all over the world. The work was dangerous but the pale horse's head was protection, although Franco had wondered aloud one day what lay beneath the violence. Ivan had explained that Thanatos was the ancient Greek personification of Death and the pale horse tattoo represented the prophecy that Death would take a quarter of the world in the end times. Franco didn't quite understand the details but it didn't matter because the tattoo was a passport to the other side of the law and a whole new level of wealth and power. That's what I've been looking for, Franco thought. That's why I'm here.

He looked around surreptitiously. There was an air of expectancy, a silence that seemed to echo around this chamber of bones. About thirty people were in the room, mostly men with a few women dotted around. He looked at one woman standing near him, her dusky features like a film star's, expensive suit in midnight blue framing her slim figure. Her shining copper hair was pinned on top of her head and a tattoo of hieroglyphics wound down beneath her clothes from the base of her neck. Franco wondered why she was here, what deeds she had performed in the name of Thanatos. She wore a black mask, as all of them did, but when her gaze met his, her eyes were like a frozen river. He looked away quickly, understanding that some deeds were not as base as a fist to the head and evil could walk in stiletto heels. Franco's glance angled away as if he had never been looking at her.

Suddenly, the atmosphere in the room changed and the rustling of clothes indicated the movement of people parting. A tall man climbed the raised dais to stand in front of the altar. He wore a long dark robe with a mask of black silk molded tightly to his face. Only the top echelons knew the true identity of the man who embodied Thanatos. Franco knew that this was the dark Master they all served, and tonight he would pledge his own allegiance. Thanatos raised his hands.

"You are the chosen few and this is a landmark event. You are part of the turning of the hands of time, for tonight I will send you out to usher in the prophecy. It has taken years to build the network we have in place but now we are ready to release the pale horse of Death into this world. Soon the

Devil's Bible will be returned to this altar. That moment will mark the beginning of the end, for the words in that book will finally fulfill the Revelation and tonight you will witness the re-enactment of the birth of Thanatos."

Franco listened intently. None of this had seemed important as money had grown fat in his bank account but it seemed that events might now be escalating.

"For those of you at the ceremony for the first time, I tell our story so that you may understand," Thanatos continued. "For those who have stood faithful with me over time, I tell this story to renew your strength and purpose in the prophecy."

He strode to one end of the dais and Franco saw the audience lean towards him, eager for his words.

"Abraham was beloved of God and was promised a son even though he and his wife were old. He was promised that endless generations would stem from his seed. He believed that God would keep this promise. Even as his bones grew weak and he stumbled to tend his sheep, he knew that God would be faithful. His God would not let him down."

Thanatos now walked to the other side of the dais and looked further into the crowd. Franco felt his gaze like a jolt of electricity. He was energized by this man and moved closer to hear more clearly.

"God did bless Abraham with a son, Isaac, dearly beloved and precious to his father. Abraham prayed daily that he would grow to be a great man and fulfill the words of his God. But one day God told Abraham to take his son to the top of Mount Moriah and there to sacrifice him."

There was a silence, a collective breath held in the crypt of bones.

"What kind of God is this, that demands the sacrifice of children?" Thanatos said, his voice soaring in the chamber. "And what kind of father was Abraham to do his bidding? But a man of faith would not back down from that direct order from on high. Obedience to God was of the highest importance. So Abraham took his son Isaac to the mountain and tied him down, even as the boy shook with fear. Tears ran down his cheeks as he begged for his life. Abraham wept and pleaded with God, but no reply came. Abraham raised the knife."

A pause. Thanatos looked around at the crowd. They waited expectantly although Franco sensed they knew what was coming.

"God sent a ram into a nearby thicket and its cries stopped Abraham from the killing stroke. God had provided another sacrifice which Abraham slaughtered in his son's place. Abraham raised his hands and cried out his thanks. He wept at God's mercy. "

Thanatos turned, beckoning into the darkness behind the altar. A stocky man dressed in the same mask and black robes came forward carrying a child tied by hands and feet. Franco could see that it was a young boy, maybe five years old. Tears and snot had crusted on his tiny face, soaking a gag wrapped about his mouth and his eyes were vacant as if he had been drugged. A gasp broke the silence. Franco realized it had come from his own throat.

"But this was in the past," Thanatos continued. "Today we stand for another form of obedience. A generation ago, my father was the one called to sacrifice his son. He heard the voice of God and believed that it was as Abraham's challenge. He worshipped here in this church. His faith was as Ezekiel's. He saw the valley of dry bones come back to life. He saw the resurrection coming through the skeletal remains of this place."

The stocky man came forward and laid the child on the altar, securing the bonds so he was tied there securely. The boy lay still, unresponsive.

"My father brought his son here, the child he loved above all else. He laid him on the altar just as this boy lies here now and he offered his child to God. He called out, pleading for God to provide another sacrifice, for a way out of the obedience that was required. Sometimes God sends another but sometimes He will ask of us that which we love the most. There must be sacrifice for then He will provide a greater blessing. So my father took up the blade."

Thanatos drew a knife from the leather sheath at his waist. Its handle was polished bone made of metacarpals, finger bones curving down to a thin wicked blade. It glinted as he held it up.

"He called one last time for God to relieve him of his burden."

Franco could hear the man's voice breaking with emotion, for he was truly reliving the moment of agony.

"But God did not speak and my father was obedient to the end."

Franco watched as the knife arced down. Even as he thought that it would stop, that this was just a crazy re-enactment of some guy's nightmare, he saw real blood spurt as the knife slammed into the little boy. He was witnessing the murder of a child in a church, a holy place. Franco started forward, as if to try and stop it. He felt Ivan's hands holding him back and then other vice-like grips as men around him realized he was trying to stop the kill. Franco watched in horror as blood ran from the child's body and dripped from the altar to the floor. The woman near him licked her lips and he could see her breathing heavily with excitement. Thanatos turned again to the audience, the bloody knife held out in front of him.

"My father sacrificed his beloved son and tonight, you are part of this call to obedience. You will join me in the renewal of life to these bones. You are the resurrection of my father's faith. For God was faithful and gave him another son and I was born to fulfill the prophecy of the end times. Tonight you will join me in obedience."

Thanatos handed the knife to the man at the altar and without hesitation, the man plunged it into the tiny body. Franco could only hope the child was dead from the first deep thrust or the shock. People moved towards the altar, crowding in their hurry to join the rite. No one spoke and Franco found himself pushed forward towards the child's body. It was a conspiracy of silence, of capitulation and the masks they hid behind prevented the assumption of responsibility for their actions. They were one crowd, a mob united by this dark force. The words of Thanatos mesmerized them and the rewards that they received in the material world kept them obedient. He bound them to him with blood and money, the most ancient chains of all and the hardest to break. Franco watched as one by one, the masked devotees stepped forward, took the knife and stabbed the child. Some thrust hard and others seemed reluctant but they all obeyed. He saw the slim woman take her turn. She took the knife from Thanatos, her fingers brushing his for just a fraction too long. She stepped into the pooling gore in front of the altar and thrust the knife in with no hesitation.

Ivan pushed Franco to the front until he stood, staring at the proffered knife.

"There is only obedience here," Thanatos said. His eyes were of a man who saw the darkness in the soul of the world, and Franco realized that he was in too deep. He couldn't go back. This man knew what he had done, knew the depths to which he had sunk, and there was only one way towards a dark redemption. Franco took the knife and stepped to the altar. Looking down, it was as if this was no longer a small person, just a skin bag of leaking blood, the face pale and the spirit gone. Franco lifted the knife a little way and asked forgiveness from the God he thought he had long forgotten. Then the blade came down one more time.

CHAPTER 5

Vlassky Dvur Castle, Kutna Hora, Czech Republic. 1.16am

THE ANCIENT HALLWAYS OF Vlassky Dvur castle were the closest Milan Noble had to a family home. It wasn't far from Sedlec and was his retreat after he played his role as the personification of Thanatos. He had little time to come here anymore since the international headquarters of Zoebios were in Paris and New York. As a pharmaceutical and health technology company it was the perfect foil to the dark underworld of Thanatos. Business had taken him away from his physical ancestry, albeit for the necessary purpose of building a platform for the fulfillment of the prophecy. Milan was glad to return now, a brief window of solitude in his busy schedule. Time seemed to be speeding up now that the plans were beginning to mature. With the teams deployed, it was only a matter of time until the prophecy could be fulfilled and he was finally released from his burden.

Milan shrugged off his black robes and left them pooled on the dusty floor by the door. He threw the black mask down next to them and switched on a lamp that cast terracotta shadows across the wood paneled walls. The glow illuminated a portrait of Arkady Novotsky. Milan had anglicized his name to Noble, a necessary break from his father's scattered past. He stepped up to the photo, a portrait of pain in sepia tint.

"I still obey you, Father," Milan said, his voice echoing in the empty hall. "Even in death, I do your will, and we are so close to fulfillment now."

He shook his head to clear the shadows that clouded his memory and walked to the end of the long dark corridor. His father had purchased the castle after a particularly successful archaeological dig. His side business of smuggling antiquities finally paid off enough to buy this grand old place. It was said to have belonged to an ancestor of theirs but Milan knew his father often had delusions of grandeur and the truth was frequently obscured by layers of fiction. His father had kept the castle private, but Milan had opened it up to the public. Most of the grounds were now managed for tours but he kept this tiny corner as his own personal space. No one was allowed to come here, not even a cleaner. As he walked, Milan shed more of his outer layers, so he was naked by the time he reached the door of the cellar. A simple white kimono hung there which he shook out and put on. With bare feet, he stepped onto the stairs leading down and shut the door firmly behind him.

Milan locked the heavy door from inside. He rested his head against the deeply grained wood, the darkness broken only by a chink of light from under the door. He breathed deeply, calm beginning to permeate through him even as the cold of the cellar prickled his arms. This place had always been his refuge, where he had run when his father rampaged in anger. This was where he had hidden when Arkady had beaten his mother to death, her screams muted through the thick wood as he shook in fear on the top step. Strangely, it had been his father who had shown him what to do at the first signs of violence. He had taught the young Milan to lock himself inside the cellar and to wait for the clock to turn a full twelve hours. Only then was it safe to come out, as the storm of his father's anger would have passed.

When his breathing had finally slowed, Milan flicked on the lights, then turned and walked down into the cellar. The lighting was low and muted, a forest green tinge from the dim light bulbs and the bonsai that grew down here, each stunted plant in its own ceramic pot. Over the years, Milan had built this precious collection and the ecosystem of lights and water that sustained them down here in an artificial world. It was an Eastern interest that stood a long way from the Christian religious tradition he was steeped in. He thought it was probably a form of rebellion against his father, recognizing in the exactness of the bonsai a way to separate a part of himself from the work he carried out in the name of the prophecy. Bonsai was about control. It focused on making the form of the tree into an interesting shape without leaving a trace of the process. His bonsai were mounted on an ancient door laid on darkly oiled stumps, eight perfectly formed mini trees in a garden that no one else would ever see.

Milan walked around the table, his hands caressing the trees, fingertips gently feeling the health of his plants. He hovered and then chose. This one was his favorite, but today he had to atone for the death of the boy. It was only fitting that he use this, his most faithful friend. The bonsai was a Chinese bird plum grown in the 'moyohgi' style, an informal upright with twisting trunk. Milan traced the curves of the tiny frame, seeking just the right spot. He turned to the tool table where his instruments were laid out in neat rows of screws, twisting wire, pliers and sharp cutters. Like the picture in the attic of Dorian Gray, these trees were the outward reflection of his inner self, a physical manifestation of the evil he committed. He warred with himself over the deeds he performed, but he knew that the culmination of the prophecy was righteous. He came here to atone, for punishment must be handed out for the sin of murder and these were his scapegoat trees.

His movements knocked some of the tiny flowers onto the carpet of rich earth. With a little implement, Milan raked the miniature garden until the soil covered them again. Bonsai were hardy trees, grown to survive the shaping by wire and vice but he had developed the hammering of nails himself, based on something he had seen in Afghanistan. Milan thought back to when his father had taken him on a trip, a rare chance to be part of an archaeological dig in a part of the world generally not visited by Westerners. They had stopped on the outskirts of a remote village and he had been surprised to see an old woman weeping as she hammered thick nails into the trunk of a tree. As she sank to her knees in front of it, he had asked the guide what she was doing. It was a scapegoat tree, he had said. It took the sins of the people and was symbolically cast out away from them. It removed their sin and suffered in silence while they carried on with their lives.

His father had then told him of the ancient Israelite practice of scapegoating where a goat took the sins of the people and was cast out into the desert, dying far from the tribe that had committed the crime. The nailing of sin to a tree was also reminiscent of the sacrifice Jesus made for the sin of mankind. It was a way of repenting and atoning without the self-harm associated with taking the punishment upon oneself. Milan had kept that memory safe and now replicated the scapegoat trees here in miniature, creating this little world of atonement hidden from the world. The trees were precious to him and to hurt them was to punish himself. He couldn't cut himself, as that was a sign of weakness. He needed to be a strong leader, to show no remorse in the face of what Thanatos must do to fulfill the prophecy. But down here, he retreated to a space where he could face his sin and acknowledge his flawed humanity. This is my prayer, he thought.

Milan selected a short fat nail from an old tobacco tin

he had found as a young man in the wasteland behind the castle. It had been thrown from a car. He fancied it was a message from the people who might have rescued him, but they never came back. Picking up a tiny hammer, he took the nail and braced it against the trunk of the Chinese bird plum. His stomach was churning and he felt nauseous as he prepared to violate the wood. It was an abuse of the sacrament of bonsai, but he had to do it and he knew the relief that came after the sacrifice. He drove the nail hard into the trunk. It only took two strikes and it had pierced the heart of the plum. Milan knelt by the tree, the flagstones hard and cold on his knees.

"I'm sorry," he whispered. "I'm so sorry."

His fingers once again traced the trunk, the smooth wood now desecrated with the nail. He stroked the tree and felt the raised bumps of other nails that had been hammered here over the years. Looking over his collection, he could see little space left for new nails as the trunks were pock-marked with silver studs. Here was the accumulation of his sin, the testament of his guilt. But Milan breathed more easily now and his calm returned. It was time now to focus on the fulfillment of the prophecy.

DAY 2

CHAPTER 6

MORGAN WOUND DOWN THE window and breathed the familiar air as the taxi skirted the city of Jerusalem and headed for the hill where the Ezra Institute overlooked the Kidron Valley. Olive groves on the hills were a dusty green, like army fatigues laid down on the earth. Morgan remembered how she had been so idealistic once, so willing to believe there could be a lasting peace in Israel. After all, people are people. They love their children, they just want to work and be happy. But over that layer of simplicity was a web of politics, religious fervor and a desire for revenge that built up two sides of a dispute that surely would never be settled.

She had spent years arguing with colleagues over the inherent goodness of people, the importance of the freedom to work, of education, equal rights for women and political democracy on both sides. Elian had been at her side for many of those arguments, smoking Noblesse and drinking his favorite Clos de Gat Har'el Syrah. She could still remember the taste of grapes and smoke when he kissed her. Morgan rubbed the back of her neck, willing the images away for this wasn't the time to be melancholy. Elian was lost to her but he had believed in her strength and in what she could achieve. A passionate man, Elian had died as violently as he had lived. Perhaps they wouldn't have made it through the fiery arguments, but now she would never know. Their love had been frozen forever that day on the Golan Heights and he was a hard man to replace. An image of Jake Timber, the ARKANE agent, suddenly came to Morgan's mind, torn shirt on a muscled back, framed by the fires of Pentecost. As he turned she saw ash on his face and his tawny eyes alight with the flames. She sighed. Clearly it was time to get a date.

The taxi pulled into the gates of the Ezra Institute and after paying her fare, Morgan stepped out into the yard. It looked more like a prison from the outside and it seemed impossible for a patient to escape as Dinah had said. Morgan was here officially here as an Oxford University psychologist who specialized in the psychology of religion. With her years of experience she could definitely justify her presence as a consultant. The door buzzed, clicked open and Dinah stood framed in the metal doorway. She beckoned Morgan through and enfolded her friend in a warm embrace.

"I've missed you. It's been too long." Dinah's strong arms crushed Morgan's slender figure to her own abundant curves.

"You too, Di."

For a moment, they just stood there, hugging. There was so much history between them and Morgan felt like she'd come home to a beloved sister. Dinah broke away and poked at Morgan's waist.

"You're too skinny. What have you been doing with yourself?"

Morgan laughed.

"Feed me later. Let's see this cell."

"Always the workaholic." Dinah looked serious. "But we need to be careful. Some of the people here know more than they're letting on. The razor blade Abraham used has disappeared and no one seems keen to investigate how he got hold of it in the maximum security wing. It's as if there is an active cover-up going on and I'm worried, Morgan. But come, I'll show you Abraham's room."

They walked through the scrubbed halls of the Institute, past the wards of beds and interview rooms.

"It seems like you have more funding than when I was last here. What's changed?" Morgan asked.

"The Israeli government withdrew all funding a few years ago," Dinah said. "We had some money from religious groups, but they had a restrictive agenda. Now we get the bulk of our money from Zoebios."

Morgan raised an eyebrow.

"Do you know of them?" Dinah asked.

"I'm just beginning to hear about their work," Morgan replied. "What do they provide here?"

She noted the well stocked cupboards along the corridor and how clean the place looked. The last time she'd been there, the corridors were dark and run down.

"They provide bulk funding for the doctors and even pay my salary, as well as sending medication. "

"And what do they want in return?" Morgan asked.

"Data. They use the information from Ezra in their global studies on health and well-being. We've been part of their neuroscience trials focused on anxiety."

"It sounds like you've drunk the Kool-Aid on this one."

"Still the cynic, Morgan?" replied Dinah. "But perhaps I have. I've gotten so tired struggling for funding all the time and it's good to know we have long term support in Zoebios. They've funded several of my projects and they also offer sabbaticals at their other global sites. I'm considering taking a post at a clinic in South Africa, just for a change. Not so many Isaiahs and John the Baptists down there."

Dinah laughed, but her smile faltered as they arrived at the secure wing.

"This is … was … Abraham's room."

Morgan looked through the square glass window.

"He was a special patient of mine," Dinah continued. "I'd done a lot of individual work with him. I thought he was getting better, but then this. Something tipped him over the edge, and at the same time, Daniel threw himself from the Western Wall. Two suicides in one day. It's unbelievable." Dinah shook her head.

"Can we go in?" Morgan pushed at the door.

Dinah glanced down the hall where an orderly was wheeling a patient. Morgan could sense her friend was wary, afraid of what might be overheard, but she had come all this way to help. Dinah unlocked the door and they entered the room, now spotlessly clean and smelling of bleach and disinfectant. Dinah pointed at the wall above the metal bed.

"You can still see the faint lines of the image. We can't get it all off and we need to paint over it. Abraham drew it in his own blood, Morgan." Dinah's voice was bereft. "I can still see his face when he said that God told him to kill himself. I feel like I've failed him, and I'm scared for the others. They're vulnerable and they're in my care."

"It's OK, Di. We'll figure this out. We always do."

Morgan studied the outline on the wall. She had the original pictures that Dinah had emailed on her phone but they hadn't adequately shown the scale. It was a life-size horse, rearing up with nostrils wide and flaring in wild abandon. On its back was the rider of death. She had seen this image before in the pale horse tattoo of Thanatos.

"What's going on?" she whispered, studying the surface of the drawing. This had to be connected to the group who had pursued her across the world for the Pentecost stones, but why might they be interested in this Institute? A community of mentally disturbed people on the outskirts of a city turbulent with religious fervor. What was she missing? Morgan went to Abraham's desk, an old wooden table and chair that looked like one she had used at school. There was an mp3 player on the desk, its green chrome surface unmarked. It looked new, a contrast to the aged wood it sat upon.

"Are the patients allowed audio?" she asked Dinah, who was now sitting on the bed, her face haggard and drawn.

"Yes, that's part of the study Zoebios is doing here. It's a combination of drug trial paired with audio stimulation."

"So where are the headphones?"

"There's a special headset that goes with the audio program. Maybe someone took it back to the storage area. It uses deep trans-cranial stimulation and it's been shown to reduce depression and improve mood. We've been trialling them for Zoebios in recent weeks."

Morgan turned to her friend, her voice urgent.

"Di, I need to see them. Trans-cranial stimulation has also been used to invoke visions of God. Remember the Persinger God helmet we studied?"

Dinah looked up.

"Of course, but these headphones are nothing like that. They're just slightly bigger than usual. The God helmet used by Persinger was more like a motorcycle helmet covered in electrodes. Anyway, I thought it didn't even work."

Morgan turned back to look at the outline on the wall.

"Certain types of people did sense a presence physically near them in the room during the study. Those with religious leanings believed it was God or sometimes Satan, so it might be relevant. Could you get me one of those headsets? I want to listen to what's on this mp3 player."

Dinah rose slowly from the bed, her back hunched and taut with stress. Morgan could see the toll this situation was taking on her friend. Dinah went back into the corridor and Morgan heard her footsteps recede down the hallway. The Dinah she knew was fast and active, but these steps were slow and heavy. She frowned and returned to her search of the room. Aldous Huxley's book 'The Doors Of Perception' sat on a shelf and a quote from the book was stuck to the wall. *"Maybe this world is another planet's hell."* Morgan smiled wryly. She had this book on her own bookshelf. She felt a flash of compassion for the dead man. In other circumstances would she be the one shut in an institute like this?

She heard a click from behind her.

Morgan turned to see the door shut and a brief glimpse of a face staring in at her. She rushed to the door to find it locked. She banged on it, shouting for Dinah. Then an explosion rocked the building.

CHAPTER 7

MORGAN BRACED HERSELF AGAINST the door as chunks of masonry fell from the ceiling. She ducked to the floor, covering her head and then rolled under the metal bed to protect herself. She could hear patients' screams above the cacophony of the alarm. Where was Dinah? Was she safe?

Another explosion, closer now. But this time the door buckled as the door frame broke and Morgan saw her chance to escape. Struggling out from under the bed, she grabbed the old wooden chair by the desk and smashed it against the wall. The chair broke apart as she focused her energy into the blow. Morgan wedged the leg into the crack in the door which had opened up in the blast. She used it as a lever until the lock mechanism broke and splintered, weakened as it was by the blast. Morgan forced the door back until she could slip through.

The corridor was full of panicked patients and nurses trying to keep them calm while leading them out of the building. Smoke was pouring into the corridor and there were visible flames at the far end. Morgan knew it wouldn't be long until the fire caught hold and the whole building would be destroyed. She grabbed the arm of a passing nurse and shouted,

"Where do you keep the headsets for the patients? Where's your storage area?"

"We need to get out. Please help me with the patients."

The nurse was clearly in shock but Morgan had to find Dinah.

"Which way?" she shouted at the woman, shaking her. The nurse pointed towards the flames.

"It's back there, but you can't go now, the fire is too close."

But Morgan was already sprinting down the corridor. As the smoke made it harder to see and breathe, she dropped to her hands and knees. Covering her mouth with a discarded robe, she crawled onwards as the blazing heat threatened to push her back. Through stinging eyes, she saw a doorway open on her left and through the smoke, the shape of a body. Dinah was lying on the floor, her head bloody. It looked like she had been attacked before the explosion.

Morgan grabbed a sheet from the pile in the storeroom and laid it down. She rolled her friend onto it. Then she spotted a number of headsets with oversized earpieces in a box marked with the Zoebios logo. But there was no time to examine them now. Taking the end of the sheet, Morgan began to crawl back down the corridor, dragging Dinah's body behind her, grateful that the linoleum meant she could pull the body easily on the slippery surface.

The smoke was heavy and thick now, billowing near the ceiling with flashes of flame shot through it. Morgan knew that the gases were building up to the point where there would soon be another explosion. They had to get out. She took another breath from the air close to the floor and then stood up, eyes squinting. She had more leverage standing, but had to hold her breath in order not to inhale the gases. Drawing on her last reserves of energy, Morgan pulled Dinah faster down the corridor, until they turned a corner and the air began to clear. At the end was a door opened to the courtyard beyond. Re-energized now, Morgan ran for it, pulling her friend to safety. They were spotted by firemen who were entering to tackle the flames and who helped them to safety.

Three ambulances with lights flashing stood in the yard outside the block. The patients who were still standing were being helped further away from the building. A paramedic moved to take the sheet from Morgan's hand but she clutched it tighter, unwilling to let Dinah out of her sight.

"It's OK," the young paramedic said. "You can let go now. We'll help your friend."

Coughing and retching from the smoke, as her eyes streamed, Morgan finally relented and let go. She watched as they lifted Dinah onto a stretcher, briefly assessed her and began wheeling her to an ambulance. Morgan sat down on the pavement and breathed from the oxygen mask they had given her. She looked back towards the wards of the Ezra Institute, flames curling from the windows up the walls, the noise of roaring as fire consumed the building. The old furnishings, linen supplies and even the paint meant the fire caught quickly. People around her were talking about a bomb attack, perhaps the Palestinians or an extremist religious group. But Morgan knew this wasn't a coincidence. There had to be a connection between the deaths of the men, the prophecy and this explosion. Perhaps it was a way to silence a particular doctor from investigating just a little too thoroughly.

Dinah.

Morgan had lost sight of where they had taken her.

She stood, looking around in desperation, oxygen mask discarded by her side. In that moment, she saw the orderly who had been in the corridor just before the explosions. He was getting into the back of the ambulance that Dinah had been put in. Heart racing, Morgan looked for a way to stop the vehicle before it drove off. She knew the man would finish what he had started if that door closed.

Behind her, a policeman was taking a statement and, like all Israeli police, he had a handgun in his belt. She knew the Jericho 941 semi-automatic would be enough to stop the man, if she could use it in time. Spinning round, she caught the policeman off guard and unclipped his gun in one movement. Morgan ran towards the back door of the ambulance as she aimed the weapon. The policeman pursued her, shouting at his colleagues to bring her down.

Morgan could see the ambulance door closing and the face of the orderly as he grinned in triumph. He was hurrying to close the door, kicking away the other paramedic who had been helping, all pretense now gone. She had to take the shot before the police stopped her or Dinah would be lost. In those milliseconds, Morgan took advantage of the tunnel vision and slowed time that adrenalin provides. She fired. One, two shots through the gap of the door. Seeing the orderly drop in the back of the van, she threw the gun to the ground and herself to her knees. Arms up, palms out in surrender, showing the weapon was gone.

"I'm IDF" she shouted. Police surrounded her, guns pointing straight at her head.

CHAPTER 8

Zoebios Head Office. Paris, France. 9.24am

THE SUBJECT WAS A forty-two year old accountant professing a moderate Catholicism that involved going to confession twice a year. He had estimated two out of ten for the importance of religious experience in his life. Of course, these questions were hidden in a raft of others that ensured the subject couldn't prepare for the experience and had no expectation of what they might feel. Dr Maria Van Garre was nevertheless experiencing a thrill of anticipation, as they only had a few more subjects to complete the research. Already the results were clear and tomorrow she would present them to the Board. The trials on the audio for anxiety and depression had been successful and fast-tracked to public release. But her academic drive had urged her to take the technology further into the realms of direct influence on behavior. She was fascinated by how far the obedience studies could be taken and now sought additional funding for the next step.

"Is that comfortable?" She adjusted the eye mask to make sure the cotton wool padding was tight against the subject's eyes. "It's important that you can't see anything."

"That's fine. So what should I be expecting?"

"It's a completely individual experience, Mr … " Maria checked the clipboard.

"Agineux."

"Of course. You should just relax and let whatever happens, happen. Just be an observer."

"But it won't hurt?"

"Of course not. The field is actually weaker than a fridge magnet," Maria replied in a soothing tone, trying not to sound like she did this several times a day. "I'm going to put the helmet on you now and then you won't be able to hear me anymore. Once it's in place, just lie back and relax. You'll hear rainfall at first as a way to help you focus. Just concentrate on breathing evenly and enjoy having a rest. I'll squeeze your hand before I leave the room so you'll know the experiment is about to begin and I'll come and get you afterwards."

"Beats a few hours at work anyhow." The man smiled, but his blinking eyes betrayed his nerves.

Maria put the helmet over his head and he pulled it into place so it fitted snugly. She fastened the strap under his chin, ensuring the markers were in the correct place to focus the weak magnetic field onto the temporal lobe. She helped him lie back and then squeezed his hand. Walking to the door, she turned the lights off, checking the room for any ambient light and then left. The subject was left in pitch darkness, snug in his relaxing chair. Some days Maria just wanted to sink into the chair herself and soothe away her stress. She had a lot of work ahead but the research was worth every second.

Her assistant, Simone Moreau, clicked on the introductory soundtrack as soon as Maria closed the door behind her. They were experimenting with different conditions for the auditory feed while leaving the magnetic field the same. Some would hear just the rainfall and thunderstorms in the distance, a relaxing soundtrack of nature. Others were fed binaural beat technology that included a behavior for them to physically perform after the experience. It was a simple task but not something they would perform without some kind of direction. Neither of the researchers knew which condition the computer would assign this subject to. It was all randomized by the program.

"Do you want to classify some of the other records while we wait for this one?" Simone asked. "I know you want the report to be ready as soon as possible."

It took around an hour for the program to complete and then they had to debrief the subject, which involved a recorded interview. They were trying to classify the experiences so that the results could be analyzed further. Maria nodded and sat down at the desk.

"Sure, let's do a couple. What have you got?"

Simone read from a printout.

"This one experienced a sudden wave of darkness and saw a distant point of light, then felt a presence standing behind, watching over them. Oh wait, they described it as 'The' Presence, not just 'a' presence."

"Ok, how did the presence feel?"

Simone skimmed the page.

"It wasn't threatening, but it wasn't kind either. It was just there."

"Tag that one with tunnel because it sounds similar to the near death experiences, and also tag with ambivalent presence. Did they hear anything?"

"Nothing noted."

Maria tutted.

"Sometimes I don't think we're asking the right questions. But it's so hard to try and put an experience into language. What else?"

"This one ticked the box indicating that the experience didn't come from their own mind, so I'll tag with external locus."

The metronomic needle on the brainwave readout swished as it changed the depths of the peaks and troughs.

"Looks like our man just had his first experience," Maria noted.

Simone shuffled through the papers. "Interesting. This woman saw flames and said she actually felt heat although it didn't burn her. She saw faces distorted by the heat and said she actually counted the individual presences as if they had been standing there next to her."

"That could be disturbing," Maria noted. "Imagine if you had that type of vision in a church or by yourself in your room at night. It's certainly the basis for nightmares."

"Or even a belief in demons and hell," Simone replied. "I know we're not meant to use religious terminology but seriously, flames? I'd be worried."

Of course they had both been in the helmet themselves but neither of them talked about their experiences. They didn't want to bring a bias to the experiment in terms of acknowledging their own belief, or lack of it. Maria knew that everyone experienced different things, which made it all the harder to classify. Those who had some form of religious belief often had visions that fitted their idea of God. Some people experienced nothing at all. They were often disappointed, as if there was something deficient in them that prevented a higher level of consciousness.

"What about the drug arm at the clinics? I'm keen to know how that went," Maria asked.

"They're wrapping up next week, although they used the modified headsets for a more portable environment. Have you tried them?"

Maria thought about the nights she had been using them as a sleep aid. It had become a kind of addiction for her and now she couldn't sleep without them. She had used a certain frequency and then a suggestion for deep sleep in the binaural beat.

"No, I'll wait for the results, but it looks promising so far."

Simone nodded.

"If they work, the Board will definitely give us funding. This could be a major breakthrough."

Maria grinned, pleased with her enthusiasm.

"Who would have believed that a simple headset could pave the way to the kingdom of heaven?"

"Do you really believe that?" Simone's voice was serious now.

Maria considered her words. These experiments were challenging for all of the researchers involved and she knew many, herself included, were wrestling with personal doubts.

"There are two positions and I flip between them. One is that God gave us this part of our brain so we could experience Him and a type of consciousness that we don't access in everyday life. The other is that we have evolved to believe in a God who doesn't actually exist but is, in fact, manufactured by our brains. I know believers and atheists who both think the God helmet validates their opposite positions."

"I don't understand why humans would evolve to believe in God if he, or she, didn't exist," Simone said. "Where's the sense in that?"

Maria shuffled the scientific papers in front of her, unsure how far to take the discussion.

"Evolutionary psychologists have suggested that perhaps mankind evolved to a point where they understood the inevitability of physical death. There were some who started to believe there was more than just a physical life, and over time, these people were selected for, in a Darwinian sense, as they were the most hopeful and the ones who helped others."

"To reduce the anxiety of death, we came up with the unending beyond the physical. Ok, I can see that." The machine pinged. Simone turned to check the display. "The subject is almost cooked. Who's doing this debrief?"

"I'll do it. You've done more than your fair share recently," Maria gathered a question sheet and a small soft toy rabbit from the pile near the door. When the light above the door went green, she stepped into the room and flicked on the low lighting. She put the toy rabbit within reach of the man but under the chair she sat down on so it wasn't obvious. She touched his hand so that he would know the experience was now over. He tried to pull the helmet off and she slowed him, helping him carefully and removing the eye pads. He blinked at the lights, his breathing elevated.

"Man, that was weird," he said, his eyes dazed.

"If you would just try to breathe gently, Mr Agineux," Maria said. "I'd like to ask you some questions about what you experienced. This is being recorded, so please be as honest as you can with your responses."

"Of course. I'm keen to find out what the hell you did to me."

"Can you start by explaining what happened at the beginning of the experience?"

Agineux leaned forward.

"It was dark and then I started to see shapes swirling about me in a kind of mist. They were like ghosts or maybe angels but they had flat faces, like nothing was really in there."

He leaned further forward, reaching under Maria's chair at full stretch. He pulled out the toy rabbit and hugged it tightly to his chest.

"I could hear voices coming from them, but I couldn't make out the words. Were those angel voices?"

Maria remained impassive.

"Please continue describing the experience," she said evenly.

"They swirled around me and then I felt more of a dominant presence, a one-ness but I was part of it too." His hands had begun to worry at the rabbit's ears, twisting them, winding and pulling them.

"I could smell something funny, maybe smoke, maybe incense. It was sticky."

"Sticky?"

"Like it got stuck in my nose, like pollen makes you clog up." At this, he gave a violent tug and ripped the rabbit's ears off, leaving a lump of pink fur in his big hands.

"Oh, sorry, I don't know what I was doing."

"That's fine," Maria said, taking the pieces from him and putting them out of sight.

"Please finish describing what you experienced."

It must be the rabbit condition again, thought Maria. She and Simone didn't know who was assigned to it, but it became obvious soon after the interview began. Suggestions were deeply embedded so the subject didn't know what they had been told to do, but the experience of the voices made it sound as if the command had come from God himself.

"It was like I was dreaming, but also awake," Agineux continued. "I've heard of lucid dreaming, perhaps that was it?"

He was looking at her for some kind of sign.

"Go on." She remained impassive.

"That was it mostly, except I wanted to stay there even though it was uncomfortable. There was something timeless about it, something that makes coming back to my daily life seem quite pointless. I want that feeling again, Doctor. How can I get it back?"

"Thank you, Mr Agineux. I appreciate your candor but we can only have you in the experiment once." She handed him a booklet. "This explains the science behind the helmet and there is also a number for you to call if you are worried or have any concerns. My assistant will show you to the rest area now."

"Isn't there some kind of personal use device for this?" he asked, a tinge of desperation in his voice.

Maria looked at him, curious about his interest.

"We have your details so we'll keep you posted with any developments. Thank you again for your time."

She walked out the room, trying to hide her elation. He had performed the rabbit action so the suggestion was embedded, but he also wanted more. If there was some kind of addictive effect that made people want to return repeatedly to the headset, that would drive additional benefits. This was the final result she needed for the Board presentation the following day.

CHAPTER 9

Central Police Station. Jerusalem, Israel. 12.41pm.

LIOR AVIDAN ENTERED THE interrogation room holding a cup of coffee and waved at the other officers to leave. He sat across from Morgan, her hands cuffed on the metal table. He placed the cup in front of her.

"Strong black. I thought you might need it."

"You remembered."

She smiled at him, fatigue showing in her face, but that violet slash in her right eye was as vivid as ever. A flash of memory and he saw her laughing, eyes sparkling at him as the waters of the Red Sea swirled about them.

"Of course … but it's been a long time."

"How's Di?" Morgan asked.

"She's in the intensive care unit at Hadassah. Don't worry, I'll make sure she's well looked after."

Morgan visibly relaxed at the positive news of her friend.

"You've done well for yourself, Lior."

His name was soft in her mouth and it thrilled him for he hadn't heard it spoken like that for many years now. He reached for her hand but she picked up the coffee cup and drank from it. He moved his hands away again and his tone changed.

"I'm not sure even the Inspector General can get you out of this one, Morgan. What are you doing here anyway? And what happened at Ezra?"

"Is the orderly dead?" she asked, ignoring his questions. "I need to speak with him. I need to know who he's working for."

"What do you mean? He's just an orderly. He was new but he was helping Dinah. You were in shock, smoke inhalation affected your judgment." He got up quickly, throwing back the chair. "Damn you, I need a way to sort this out. It could be manslaughter if he doesn't survive."

She looked up.

"So he is alive then? I need to speak with him. Please, Lior."

He slammed his hand down on the table.

"You have no right to ask Morgan, you have no place here anymore. You left us behind, remember?"

The look of pain on her face silenced him. She had also lost someone back then. But times were always hard here and she had left to find pieces of a family she didn't even know.

"There were reasons," she said. "I didn't know how to continue here any longer, after my father died and with Elian gone. There was nothing to stay for."

Lior gave a harsh laugh.

"You had friends who loved you."

"Loved?"

"Enough," Lior brushed aside her question. "I need to know about Ezra. What happened?"

Morgan explained why Dinah had called her, what they had seen in Abraham's room, the fire and its aftermath.

"I'm sure the orderly set the fire and that he attacked Di," she explained. "There's something else going on, something that caused those suicides and now someone is trying to cover it up. I think there's a bigger plan here and we're only seeing a small part of it."

"And you think it could be this Thanatos organization, with a plan to resurrect religious extremism? It sounds a bit far fetched. Ezra counts for nothing in the world. It's a tiny hospital with no global reach. What interest would this organization have in such a place?"

Morgan took a deep breath. Lior could almost see her thinking.

"It's bigger than Ezra. You must have a team on the suicide at the Western Wall. This could help solve it."

"You're right," Lior nodded. "That's a PR disaster. How he got up there past the guards is one question. Then there are claims he was shot by the Muslim guards from the Dome of the Rock, and of course, the prophecy has been leaked."

"What prophecy?" Morgan asked, her handcuffs chinking with her agitation.

"You didn't hear the details? He was clutching the prophecy from Revelation, that a quarter of the world would die by sword, famine, plague. You know the one, you're the expert in all that religious stuff."

Morgan's face had gone pale.

"What is it?" Lior asked, concerned about her.

"It can't be ... but it must be."

"What? You need to share this information. I want to help you, Morgan, but you're not helping yourself."

"It is Thanatos; the pale horse proves it. I'm sorry, Lior, but I need you to call someone for me. You're not going to like it but they're going to get me out of here."

CHAPTER 10

Capela dos Ossos, Evora, Portugal. 11.38pm

THE STREETS OF EVORA in southern Portugal were quiet as Natasha El-Behery stepped out of the midnight blue Mercedes Benz SLS AMG Coupé. She breathed in the cool air, thankful for the darkness after the heat of the summer day. Franco and Ivan pulled up behind her in their more functional sedan and she walked to their car, turquoise rings flashing as she smoothed back her copper curls. She looked towards the church of St Francis and then bent to the window.

"Stay behind in the shadows," she said. "I'll try to get the book the easy way but be ready on my word." The men nodded. Natasha smiled, bestowing on them a flash of her favor. Like the winter sun, it was swift and brilliant, but quickly turned to a freeze.

Her heels clicked as she walked down the path towards the church, pencil slim skirt hugging her shapely legs. She knew the designer outfit was hardly suitable for a Franciscan church, but she found that her appearance made the men she sought underestimate her. She wore long sleeves in all weathers, covering scars she preferred to keep hidden from prying eyes that might question her sanity, but she knew that pain kept her on the edge of what could be achieved.

Without pain, there was no victory, she thought. She touched the newest scar, one she had cut in front of Milan to demonstrate her dedication to finding the book he sought. He had watched her cut deeply and then had licked her flesh clean of blood, before taking her with slow thrusts that seemed to match the beat of her heart.

She had found a man worthy of her devotion in Milan Noble. She knew she was his equal but she had to prove that to him before he would believe it. She didn't intend to let him treat her like the other women he so frequently bedded, so she had asked him for this special task. If she could bring him the Devil's Bible it would prove to him she could be his partner in the dark kingdom he ruled. He was obsessed with the book and the curses that were supposedly within. It was his black hope, a fixation that she would use to bind him to her.

Natasha walked under the high arches towards the crypt, the path lit by tiny lights. She had been told that it was always open, a monk on duty praying for the souls of those taken before him. As she approached, the light from inside the crypt shone a deep golden red, as if the fires of hell burned within its portals. Natasha looked up at an inscription over the door. It read 'We bones, lying here, for yours we wait.' She smiled. It was melodramatic but effective for the chapel had been built for contemplation on the transitory nature of life. We will be bones soon enough, she thought to herself, but Death didn't frighten her. Her father had brought her up amongst the ancient sites of Egypt to believe that she was better than this life. She had come to believe her inheritance was the legacy of the pyramids themselves, an everlasting life. She was brought up studying the bones of the past, but now she was in Europe to learn more about how that history could be turned into temporal power. So, for now, she would be Milan's woman while she learned all she could from him.

Natasha stalked into the crypt, her heels echoing in the
silent space. It had a low vaulted ceiling painted in white
with gold filigree and death's head motifs. The columns and
walls were decorated with long bones and skulls in patterns,
swirling around those who prayed for salvation here. A
monk knelt by the altar, head bent in prayer. Natasha walked
up behind him and he turned his head as she approached.

"May I help you?" he enquired, his voice just above a
whisper. She could see he was near the grave, wrinkles
around his watery blue eyes cut deep into a face that knew
pain and suffering.

"I'm looking for a book," Natasha said. "I heard it was
kept here."

"We have many books in the church library. Was it
something specific? The history of the crypt perhaps? We
get many scholars here."

He clearly knew she was not a scholar and Natasha
stepped closer as he tried to rise off his old knees to face
her.

"I want the Devil's Bible," she whispered, standing close
to him. His eyes closed for a moment, as if to shut out the
world. "I see you know the book. Where is it?"

The monk opened his eyes again and Natasha saw fear
restrained in his soul.

"The ones who knew are buried here," he said, "and their
bones cry out to God to keep the location secret from those
who would use its power."

Natasha reached out with one perfectly manicured fin-
gernail and scratched it down the monk's cheek.

"I don't believe you know nothing," she said. "And I will
have that book."

She turned and beckoned to the shadows. Franco and
Ivan stepped forward and the monk inhaled sharply, a
primal sound of fear.

"My friends and I will help you remember if you don't

show me where the book is," Natasha said. "Why don't you just tell us now?"

The monk began to whisper a prayer. Natasha knew he wouldn't give them the book without some persuasion. Perhaps he didn't even know where it was. No matter. He would be an example. Even if she had to get through all the monks to find the book Milan wanted, she would deliver on her promise. She looked around the crypt, eyes settling on two desiccated corpses that dangled from chains on the wall. One was a child, the other a man, but both were sacks of sagging flesh, hanging lifeless high near the ceiling. Saints perhaps, but now they would serve her dark purpose.

"Get that down," she indicated one of the cadavers to Franco. The monk prayed louder. Ivan backhanded him into silence.

Franco pulled down the ancient corpse, throwing the body to the ground, unwinding the chains that had held it up. Natasha turned to the monk.

"This will be your fate unless you tell me where the book is hidden."

He shook his head. Natasha nodded at Ivan and he punched the old man hard in the stomach, winding him. The monk went down, clutching his stomach, next to the corpse. Natasha pushed his head while he was still off balance and he fell face first onto the desiccated body, his hands sinking into dead flesh. She stepped on the back of his neck, pushing his face down into the human decay, her stiletto heel marking his skin.

"Breathe deeply," she said, her voice echoing around the crypt. "For this is what you will become."

The monk was panicking, trying desperately to get off the body. Natasha stepped back and Franco wound the chains around his wrists, pulling his arms behind his back and then began to hoist him.

"This is an ancient form of torture," Natasha said. "We'll

keep lifting and your body weight will break your arms with excruciating pain and eventually you'll suffocate. But not before I peel the flesh from your old bones."

Natasha removed a knife from her handbag and showed it to the monk, as she caressed the ivory handle. She held it out, the point towards his right eye as he tried vainly to pull away from her.

"This was given to me by my father. It's a sacrificial knife from the tomb of an Egyptian Queen, the great Hatshepsut, used for thousands of years to inflict pain and death, and to perform sacrifice."

The monk was choking with the dust from the dead body. He wheezed and coughed as Ivan began to wind the handle, pulling his hands up behind him and forcing his head downwards towards the knife as Natasha calmly held the blade towards his face.

"Where's the Devil's Bible?" she demanded. "I will torture and kill more of your brothers if you don't reveal the location to me."

The monk rasped and wheezed his reply, finding resolve deep within.

"Better is the day of death than the day of birth."

Natasha smiled. "Ecclesiastes, my favorite book. How appropriate."

She nodded at Ivan who yanked the chain hard so the monk's face was jabbed down onto the knife and it pierced the flesh under his eye. Blood poured from the wound and he moaned in pain.

"We can do this all night, you know. You have plenty of time to contemplate the scriptures and your own end." She leaned in. "Where's the book?"

The monk shook his head again. This time Natasha dragged the knife down his cheek, slowly, so blood welled up in its path. She looked into his eyes. "The dead know nothing, old man. They have no further reward, and even their name is forgotten."

He wheezed again, as blood dribbled into his mouth.

"You know the scriptures and yet you do evil to seek evil. I will not send you further into this sin."

"But you will, I will see to that. Can't you see that I love my work? I enjoy carving bodies, sculpting them." She bent and lifted the bottom of his robe. "I particularly enjoy cutting off the useless parts, the offensive parts." He was struggling now, trying to get away from her, attempting to pray but she could see from his eyes that this was his weakness. As all men, she thought. So fragile in defense of their bodies, so weak.

"Where's the book?" Natasha asked again as Ivan yanked up the chain and she stepped closer, pulling the monk's robes up and holding the knife point to his groin. The fight went from his eyes, the wheezing worse now.

"What's the use?" he said, "I'm protecting nothing but a lie told for generations. The book isn't here."

"But I was told it was sent here by the Vatican," Natasha replied with indignation.

"No doubt that confession was also given through torture," the monk said, his eyes sharper now, as if the pain had concentrated his spirit. Natasha could see she needed to finish this. Her fingernails began to caress his old thighs. She licked her lips, anticipating the pain to come.

"Before I make you as Origen, tell me, is it better for a man to cut it off than sin against his vows?"

The monk groaned. "Truly, it's not here. I don't know where they took it. I promise. But there are other ossuaries."

Natasha's eyes narrowed. "What do you mean?"

"There are other places like this, where the bones of the holy would protect such an evil book. I only know it's buried with the dead, for they cannot speak its blasphemy. Not here, but at one of the others, perhaps. Kill me," he pleaded in a hoarse voice, "but let me keep my vows intact."

Natasha could see he had nothing left to give her. He didn't know where the book was, but the trail led to other ossuaries and she had spies in place. They would find it and she would claim her reward from Milan. She bent forward to whisper in the monk's ear.

"What has been will be again, what has been done will be done again. There is nothing new under the sun."

With the last words from Ecclesiastes, she slit the monk's throat, blood spurting over her gloves as she stepped away from the pulsing gore. The monk hung on the chains, his eyes closing as death took him. Natasha turned and walked away, her heels clicking again on the stone, leaving tiny imprints of blood on the floor of the crypt.

DAY 3

CHAPTER 11

Zoebios Head Office. Paris, France 7.15am

THIS IS IT, MARIA thought as she walked into the lobby of the Zoebios building. Today I can finally present my results to the Director and the Board. Today I will make a name for myself and my research. She had to hold herself back from skipping a little as she joined the queue for the security checks. She smoothed her hands down over her neat pinstriped suit instead, appearing far more restrained than the feelings she held within. The Board had released the audio programs for anxiety and depression but she now had more extensive data that would take it even further than they expected. After the late nights and extensive preparation, today was her chance to shine. She needed the bathroom again, third time in an hour. It's just nerves, she thought, be calm.

Maria entered the elevator and ascended to the twenty-first floor. Few people spoke on the journey between floors. It had become established office practice because the building contained areas that were not accessible to all and secret projects were tacitly acknowledged but not mentioned. Drug research and health companies were often targets of industrial espionage so the code of silence meant Maria had little idea what was going on elsewhere in the company. Not that it really mattered because she was so busy on her own projects anyway.

The elevator doors opened onto the main landing, identical on every floor. Glass paneled doors with access codes and retinal scans allowed entrance only to the staff. They were emblazoned with the etched Zoebios logo, the unfurling shoot of new life. Inside, the office area and labs beyond were quiet, one of the reasons that Maria liked to come in early, even though she also worked late most nights. There was nothing to go home to and besides, she loved her work. The early morning was the time of day she felt able to think, to centre herself, and today she needed to go over the presentation for the final time. She wanted to go over the figures again, to check and recheck. Silly, she laughed to herself. She had already examined them ten times and her best scientists had retested the results. Everything was correct but her nerves still fluttered, for this day could make or break her career.

Maria walked through to her office and sat down at the desk. It was tidy, with a sleek monitor, wireless keyboard and mouse offset by a vermilion crystal paperweight her mother had given her. She took a deep breath, preparing to go through the material once again. Her gaze drifted upwards to the framed print on the wall opposite. It was a large poster of the Escher drawing, Circle Limit IV. She had always been fascinated with how Escher tessellated images to tell a fundamental truth. In this image, angels in white and devils in black opposed each other through the print, the shadow of one highlighting the other. It was a permanent reminder that both were needed to form the whole, she thought. We all have light and dark in us and the barriers between them are permeable.

There was no grey in the Escher image, only white and black, and Maria believed that all scientific research needed to be seen through this prism. So much of it could be used for good or evil purposes and she was grateful that she worked for an ethical company like Zoebios, whose focus was on improving the human population. But she acknowledged the potential diabolical uses for even her own research if it got into the wrong hands. She had accepted long ago that there were trade-offs in ethics, that animal experiments were justified to save human lives, that the abhorrent experimentation of the past informed the breakthroughs of the present. The Escher print helped her put that in perspective.

"Morning Maria." Her assistant, Simone, popped her head around the open door. "Can I get you anything?"

Maria smiled and snapped out of her Escher trance.

"Morning. No, I'm fine, thanks. Any news?"

Simone frowned. "There have been some problems with one of the clinics using the drug pairing with the new headsets. Harghada has dealt with it, apparently, but you need to know in case they bring it up."

"Yes, I got the email this morning about the suicides. It's an anomaly, I'm sure of it." Maria frowned at her watch. "Can you shut the door behind you? I just want to go over these figures one more time."

Simone nodded and backed out, closing the door behind her. Maria bent her head to review her work again, trying to distill years of effort into the short presentation, acutely aware of what was at stake.

The boardroom was on the thirty-fifth floor, just below the penthouse where the Director, Milan Noble, had private apartments. Maria had arranged with his secretary to gain access early in order to set up the presentation for the event. Everything was now ready and she stood at the window, looking out over Paris. It was a glorious day and she felt a touch of vertigo as she looked out towards the curving Seine far below. The wire outline of the Eiffel Tower reflected the sun over shimmering buildings. Fall would come soon, her favorite time, when she would feel part of the earth and the seasons again. The craziness of summer heat would give way to chill nights, warmed by wine and friends.

A door opened and voices could be heard in the lobby. Maria straightened, put on her best professional smile and watched the Board members as they entered and sat at their appointed seats, six men representing the decision-making power behind Zoebios. They spoke to each other as they entered, none acknowledging her. At one minute to ten, Milan Noble entered the room.

"Good morning, gentlemen," he said as he looked around. "Dr Van Garre, thank you for your time today. I'm looking forward to your presentation."

Maria flushed slightly.

"Thank you, sir." She chided herself inwardly. How could a mature woman such as herself feel like a schoolgirl in front of him? She checked her notes while he finished his greetings. Milan Noble made women weak and men jealous. Tall and commanding, his physical presence filled the room.

"You may begin," Milan smiled, and sat down, switching his attention fully to her. She had heard of the power of his gaze, but now she truly understood it. It was a gift, one he cultivated, and his charisma swept all before him. Maria began.

"My lab has been focusing on mental health for the last four years, specifically investigating binaural beat brain-waves and how they can be used to carry messages into the deep brain. This is the key to the new anxiety and depression treatment that has just recently been released to the public. That method has been tested and proven, but today I want to take a step further into the realms of behavior modification using the same mechanism."

Maria could see she had the full attention of the Board

members and she changed the slide to show a brain and aural apparatus used in the experiments.

"First, we went back to basics," she explained. "Binaural beats are auditory brainstem responses that originate in the superior olivary nucleus of each hemisphere. They result from the interaction of two different auditory impulses in opposite ears where the difference between the frequencies is experienced as a wave across the hemispheres. The binaural beat is not heard as you would listen to music, but it is perceived by the unconscious and can be used to communicate messages based on an alternate state of consciousness. Brain waves oscillate in the same way as tuning forks and we have access to control them through binaural beats. Until now the research hasn't been used to affect physical behavior, but our breakthrough came when we combined this with research by Persinger and also with a drug regime."

Milan Noble had been writing notes, but at this he looked up.

"I've read Persinger's research with the God helmet but how does it relate to binaural beats?"

Maria nodded her acknowledgment of the question and clicked forward to show highlights of the original God helmet research.

"For those who may be unfamiliar, Professor Michael Persinger is a cognitive specialist who has been researching neuro-theology, a specific branch of brain science that looks at religious experience and how it occurs in the brain. The original God helmet was a crude device that stimulated the temporal lobe with a weak magnetic field. Participants in the original experiments sometimes experienced visions or felt another presence in the room. But now, regardless of what an individual believes, we have been able to use the suggestion of God or the Other in our binaural experiments."

Maria looked at Milan to check for further questions but he nodded for her to continue. She felt elated at his encouraging response so she clicked the button for the next slide. It showed a Caravaggio painting in muted reds with a dark Italian landscape in the background. An old man stood holding his young son down, a knife to his throat. An angel grasped the man's hand to stay the blade as a ram nudged into the frame, awaiting sacrifice in the boy's place. Next to the image was a headline from a newspaper article that announced the assassination of Yitzhak Rabin, Israeli Prime Minister, at the hands of Yigal Amir, a right wing extremist Jew who protested against the peace accords between Israel and the Palestinians. Maria had Milan's focused attention now. He was leaning forward, his eyes fixated on the screen.

"Abraham," he said. "Why?"

"This started out as a thought experiment for me," Maria replied. "For many people, the ultimate authority is God, so I based the experiments on that principle. In 1995, Yitzhak Rabin was assassinated and his murderer said that God told him to do it. It echoes the biblical story of Abraham. If you believe that the ultimate authority is God, even if you are asked to do things you don't want to, you will perform them anyway. Even if the task is abhorrent, people will usually obey a higher authority figure. This is also demonstrated by Stanley Milgram's studies on obedience."

"Could you refresh our memories on that too, Dr Van Garre," Milan asked with a raised eyebrow.

"Of course." Maria flicked to images of subjects strapped to electric devices with voltage meters marked Extreme Danger. "Milgram was fascinated by the behavior of the Nazis during the Second World War, when ordinary people did horrific things to other humans because they were ordered to by authority figures. Many said they were just following orders and in this way they gave up personal responsibility for their actions so Milgram conducted a variety of experiments that proved that just about everyone would have done the same thing. There were many iterations of his experiment, but in essence a subject had to administer an electric shock to another person if they failed memory tests. The subject didn't know that the person being shocked was an actor, so they truly believed they were causing pain. The shocks continued to be administered at the request of an authority figure through various levels of torture through to extreme levels that would cause death. Essentially the responsibility was shifted to the authority figure. In applying that to the binaural beat research, we realized that if we could bring a sense of authority into the commands using a sense of the Other, then people would obey the embedded directives. Of course we would be asking subjects to behave in ways that were positive and healthy rather than causing pain to others which has huge potential for the weight loss industry and the obesity epidemic as well as many other possibilities."

"And have the experiments been successful?" Milan asked.

Maria smiled proudly and flicked onto the next slide to show a detailed graph.

"The results have far exceeded what we expected. You can see the various responses here from the different arms of the trial. A physical action was requested through the binaural channel, not just a thought, so we influenced actual behavior. We found that the feeling of the Other being present is particularly enhanced by the subject wearing oversized earphones that are a more portable version of the God helmet. This would also enable an easier rollout to the public."

The screen flicked to show an image of the earphones.

"Within our clinics, we were able to pair this with an enhanced drug regime, which was even more successful."

"But you have had problems as a result of the research, haven't you?" asked Dr Armen Harghada. Up to this point the subdued lighting in the conference room and the close proximity of Milan Noble meant Maria hadn't focused on the other men in the room. Harghada was Milan's right hand man and a medical doctor. His job title was nebulous but he was feared by the Zoebios staff as he was known to have a formidable memory and allegedly made problems 'disappear' for the company.

"Correct," Maria replied. "We did have some problems in one clinic. For those individuals already primed for religious mania, the suggestions can make them even more extreme. We have had two suicides in one of the clinics in Israel, where people are hospitalized with Jerusalem Syndrome. But I'm confident that with adjustments to dosage in their drug regime and changes to the audios specifically for such outliers, the research can still be used."

Harghada leafed through the pages of her report.

"You mention LSD in some of your preliminary notes," he commented. "It's a class A drug, Dr Van Garre, and not even available for medical usage. What exactly were you doing with it?"

His eyes seemed to bore into her.

"It was a hunch, sir," Maria stammered a little under his attack. "We know that LSD is a psychoactive drug that causes extraordinary shifts in consciousness with even small doses. We have conducted several small experimental studies combining its use with the audio input. We have performed the same tests with mescaline, based on Aldous Huxley's 'Doors of Perception.'"

"What's that?" one of the other men cut in. It was Nechiffe, head of accounting. Harghada rolled his eyes but let Maria continue.

"Huxley is well known for his novel 'Brave New World' but he also spent many years experimenting with various alternative states of consciousness. 'Doors of Perception' was written as a recollection of a trip using mescaline, at a time when it wasn't restricted."

"What did he see?" Nechiffe asked. "Did it work?"

"He explained the experience with the analogy of Plato's 'Being but not separated from Becoming,'" Maria replied. "This is a complicated concept for those of us who haven't experienced it but it could be described as a few timeless hours outside the world. There was no striving, just an experience of being. I was particularly interested in his description of not being concerned for survival anymore and I interpreted this experience as a way to open the unconscious further to the suggestions we might plant with binaural technology."

Harghada wasn't finished with her and cut back in.

"Huxley was on mescaline, so why LSD for your trials?"

"They're both psychoactive but mescaline leaves the subject mostly lucid and coherent, whereas LSD is character-ized by confusion and disorientation. Mescaline has a stronger euphoric effect, but it also makes people want to lie down and relax, whereas LSD is more of a stimulant. We wanted people to be able to actively behave in a way we suggested, so we needed more of a stimulant. But these were tiny trials with willing participants in a highly regulated environment. We were testing whether a variant of the psychoactive drug could be used in extreme cases to reduce the negative side effects of anxiety but still enable the behavioral response."

"And what do you see as the potential uses of this tech-nology, Doctor?" Milan asked. He was so keen to know more that Maria was sure she would be getting her research funding approved.

"In applying it to the therapies Zoebios currently offers, we could use it with schizophrenia medication to encourage self-care and override self-harm. With post-traumatic stress, we could use it for promoting well-being and preventing suicide. It could be applied to treating addiction, in helping people give up smoking or stop taking harmful drugs. It could be used to ensure people follow regimes like weight loss for obesity. These initiatives could transform healthcare as they are non-invasive and have few side effects. Taking it further, the punitive aspect could be used in prisons for sex offenders and murderers. Research has shown that these categories of subjects respect a specific and different kind of authority."

"And what are you asking for today? What is your funding proposal?"

Maria clicked the final slide.

"The next phase would be to move to more extensive trials by releasing the headsets to specific groups of people already using Zoebios' audio programs and counseling. We can also pair with the clinics to test drug regimes, with the permission of the participants, of course. I would also like to publish some papers on the research. It has far reaching implications so it can only be a good thing if the data is shared."

Milan stood, his eyes hooded as if shutters had come down on his enthusiasm. Maria felt a shift in the room. Had she asked for too much? Her confidence sank a little. She knew the amazing potential of her work, but did they recognize it?

"Thank you Dr Van Garre. We'll discuss your proposal along with some of the others made today. If you would wait in the ante-room, you will be notified shortly."

"Of course. Thank you your time today, gentlemen."

Maria unplugged her laptop, picked up her papers and walked to the door where Milan Noble's sharp nosed personal assistant waited to show her to the ante-room. Maria sat on the edge of the chair and waited.

In the Boardroom, Milan addressed the group around the table.

"Gentlemen, I think you will agree that this research isn't our core competency. Therefore it's not something I want to heavily invest in. The rollout of the audios for anxiety and depression will continue but we won't jeopardize its success with any changes. I will assign a small budget for some more experimentation, but on no account will this be made public. Persinger and the neuro-theologians are considered to be way outside the realm of science with this research. I fear it would damage our reputation to be seen dabbling in it. I will speak to Dr Van Garre later. Let's take a break now and be back here in twenty minutes for the next funding presentation. Thank you."

The board members checked their smart phones and chatted amongst themselves as they left the room, the proposal already forgotten in their busy schedules.

"Armen, would you stay please?"

The last man out shut the door, leaving the two men standing by the huge picture window overlooking Paris.

"I know what you want," Harghada said after a moment. "This is the carrier that can spread the final message of the prophecy."

Milan nodded slowly as he stared out the window. In his mind he imagined curls of smoke rising from the ancient buildings of Paris, the burning of the dead to come.

CHAPTER 12

St Martin-in-the-Fields Church. London, England. 9.13am

TOURIST CROWDS STREAMED INTO Trafalgar Square, another busy day in this glorious city as Morgan walked up the steps of St Martin-in-the-Fields. She never tired of coming to London, although her retreat would always be Oxford. This city was life in all its infinite variety. There was no stagnation, it was ever-changing. When people couldn't take the pace anymore, they had to leave, because London wouldn't wait. Its waters rushed on, drowning those who couldn't stay afloat in the myriad depths.

Morgan had walked past St Martins many times but had never actually entered. The daily concerts had tempted her, but there were always other things going on. Jake had suggested it as a place to meet, somewhere they could talk before seeing Marietti, the Director of ARKANE. After Lior had made the call to Marietti back in Jerusalem, it had taken only an hour before she had been freed although Lior had been livid at her refusal to speak further. She feared that perhaps their friendship was now over for good, but 'no regrets' was a keystone of Morgan's world and she had none now. She believed in reinvention and that meant people were inevitably left behind.

At the doorway of the church stood a block of stone,

'Word became flesh' carved on its side. On top, a newborn baby emerged from the rock, attached by its umbilical cord to the stone. Morgan stroked the side of the carving, her fingers tracing the baby's arm. It was beautiful, even though it represented something she didn't personally believe in. It seemed strange to portray God helpless as a newborn, but the symbolism of the rock was pervasive throughout Christian art and architecture. It was modern art contrasting with the traditional church in a dramatic way.

Seen from Trafalgar Square, St Martins looked more like a classical temple, with its Corinthian columns, raised dais and pediment. The British Coat of Arms stood triumphant over the door with the lion, the unicorn and the motto of the monarch, 'Dieu et mon droit', God and my right. It was completed with the motto of the Order of the Garter, 'Honi soit qui mal y pense', Shame to him who evil thinks.

The strains of a recital could be heard from within as Morgan opened the door and entered the church. At the front, near the altar, a string quartet was playing. She didn't recognize the piece but the music lifted her spirits and soothed her anxiety at seeing Jake again. She knew that this church focused on honoring God by being open and inclusive, a beacon of enlightened faith rejecting fundamentalism and enabling people to question and discover belief for themselves. The space was light and airy, lit by chandeliers in the high coffered ceiling. Carvings were picked out in gilt, the gold and ivory color scheme making the church a relaxing place. The dark wooden pews were hard and there were cushions that could be hired to soften them but Morgan chose to sit directly on the unyielding wood to gaze upwards. A second tier of seats rose above the nave on Corinthian columns, ornate capitals picked out in gold leaf. She was also surprised to see a sunburst of gold above the altar with the Hebrew letters YHWH surrounded by cloud. The God of this church was represented not just by the tiny baby outside but the invisible presence of her own all powerful, un-nameable deity. In the corner, a skeletal figure stood holding a dead child in his arms, representing the victims of injustice and violence. Behind the simple altar, a triple paneled window allowed rays of sunlight to fall on the musicians, who sat in a pool of honeyed light.

"Designed by an Iranian woman, you know."

Morgan started at the soft voice and turned to see that Jake had quietly seated himself in the pew behind her. His dark eyes also looked up at the window, amber flecks picked out like the gold in the detail of the church. Clean shaven, Jake was dressed for the office but she knew that under his smart shirt, he was a man of action.

"What do you think it means?" he asked her, leaning forward, a touch of South African heritage in his accent. Morgan noticed his clean scent and the corkscrew scar just above his left eyebrow, a twister she longed to touch. He was so close and yet there was too much unsaid between them. He had left her, betrayed her, but then he had come back and saved her life. Now it looked as if a shared enemy would bring them together again.

Morgan looked back up at the window. In the centre of the middle pane, an oval of clear glass sat on an oblique angle with black lines of steel skewed around it. They formed a vortex with lines that made an extended cross. Green trees could be seen behind, a breeze rustling the leaves outside.

"Space and time bending around the creation spirit?"

Jake smiled. "The cradled egg thrown into this angular world?"

Morgan laughed quietly. "Whatever it means, I like it."

He sat back in the pew.

"Are you really coming in, Morgan? We can find Thanatos with the new information you've provided. You don't need to join us."

Was that hesitation in his voice? Morgan couldn't read

him. But this wasn't about Jake. She needed the change and the challenge ARKANE would bring.

"I want to find Thanatos," she replied. "And I can't let you have all the fun now, can I?"

"What about the University, your practice?"

"I can't continue with the practice as it was, not after what happened at Pentecost. The deaths made news, even though I was cleared of everything. Oxford will keep me on in an honorary position and I can continue with my research at ARKANE."

Morgan paused and the sound of strings soared in the space between them.

"Are you OK with it?" she asked.

He looked directly at her, his eyes giving no hint of his true feelings, but his voice was warm.

"Of course. We made a good team before, I'm sure we can make it work again. We can find Thanatos together, and I know how much you want to get your hands on the ARKANE database." He stood. "Come on then, let's go. I'll show you around your new office."

Morgan followed Jake down some stairs to the crypt under the church and then to the very back of the low domed space where a corridor dog-legged away from the main meeting area. There, amongst brass rubbings of life-size saints and boxes of postcards, was a tiny back entrance to ARKANE. It looked like a store cupboard, completely nondescript. Jake glanced behind him to check if anyone was watching, but the corridor was empty. He swiped his card and put his eye to the retinal scanner that popped out of a side compartment. The door opened.

"Welcome back," he said. "I hope you'll stay longer this time."

His amber eyes flashed a smile and Morgan thought for a moment she saw a warmth born of their adventures together. Then he dampened it down again, returning to the professional standing they had to be on here. But the chemistry was still there. They walked down a plain white corridor towards another door at the end.

"This area has cameras and sensors tuned to biometrics so you can be recognized," Jake said.

"And I'm already in the system?"

"Of course; Spooky sorted it out for you. He's been eagerly awaiting your arrival."

The elevator door opened as they approached and inside various buttons lit up to show Jake's access. He pressed Labs and they headed down. Morgan had been shown the ARKANE vault when she had left the Pentecost stones for safekeeping but she hadn't yet experienced a full tour of the London Headquarters. She was still amazed at how large the facility was, yet it lay under one of the most famous squares in the world and was a secret known only to a few.

The ARKANE Institute was publicly recognized as an academic research centre but most outsiders had no idea about the kick-ass arm of specialist operators solving mysteries and seeking artifacts for the vault. ARKANE specialized in the intersection between science and faith, the acknowledged real and the paranormal, that which fell outside the realm of rational truth. Now Morgan had made the decision to join the team, it felt like her first day at school. She had something to prove and something to give back, especially as they had just busted her out of an Israeli jail.

"This floor is where most of the grunt work is done," Jake said. "There are labs and meeting rooms, as well as teleconference rooms to work with the other facilities."

"Other facilities?" Morgan asked.

Jake turned at her question.

"Yes, you've seen the one at the Pitt Rivers in Oxford but

we also have places all over the world in sites of particular religious or spiritual significance. Some are fully staffed like this and others are just agents working remotely. We also use the facilities of many foreign intelligence services. ARKANE holds leverage over many governments and religious organizations. That's how we got you out of Jerusalem, by the way."

"I wanted to say thank you," Morgan replied quickly.

Jake smiled and then walked down the corridor away from her.

"Don't worry, you'll no doubt repay the favor, since we'll be working so closely together now."

She heard his words but he turned away, so she couldn't quite see what he felt about that. Morgan hurried to catch him up.

"So, give me the grand tour," she said. "Then I'm keen to get on with investigating the bombing at Ezra."

Jake indicated glass paneled doors to the left and right that opened up into separate work areas.

"We've tried to modernize the layout but it was designed for another age so most of the rooms are separate. Each of these workspaces is available to the teams for study. On this level are the open labs." He stopped to look into one and beckoned for Morgan to join him.

"What are they studying here?" she asked as she looked inside. There were several researchers handling documents with tweezers and white gloves.

"They're digitizing those manuscripts for further analysis but currently this is the project room for the Mayan doomsday prophecy."

"Seriously?" Morgan's eyebrows raised in surprise.

"You don't think we could stay out of that one do you?"

Morgan laughed softly. "But you don't believe that it's going to happen, surely? ARKANE doesn't believe the world will end?"

"It doesn't matter what we think, it's what many believe. The power of belief makes people do crazy things. We have to prepare for what may happen and for how some people may react. ARKANE monitors where the craziness is likely to be so we can move to calm things down."

"I see." She paused, looking back through the window at a woman wearing a Muslim head covering. "That scientist is wearing the hijab. I thought ARKANE was primarily Christian?"

"It was originally started as a defense against those who sought to destroy Christianity, even the idea of God, with rational thought and science. But that soon evolved into an investigation of the wider paranormal. We deal with anything that has a remotely spiritual or religious connection now and so ARKANE employees come from all traditions and faiths or in fact, lack of faith. We find the different perspectives enrich the research as we investigate from different angles."

They continued walking down the corridor.

"I should think what you research here must make lack of faith impossible."

"Perhaps," Jake said, as they reached another glass door. "This is one of the more open workrooms integrated into the research system."

He showed her in and Morgan smiled in wonder. The room was wide, with a high ceiling, and a natural light suffused the walls with warm color. On the far wall, a waterfall could be seen and the sound of falling water permeated the room. There were ferns and foliage making alcove spaces for people to work in a natural and relaxing atmosphere.

"It's gorgeous, but why a waterfall?" she asked.

"We needed to do something about people being down here in the dark with no windows, so all the rooms have a virtual reality atmosphere with infused light and natural features. It means people can stay down here working for hours and not go mad." He smiled. "But of course, I have to get out of here as much as possible."

"Yes, I don't see you as much of a researcher," Morgan teased. "But how do others work here?"

Jake indicated an alcove where a young man sat. He had pulled out a screen from the wall and sat working at it.

"There are workstations built into the suite, and then we have Martin's special project over there."

He pointed at what looked like a tanning booth hidden in one corner, landscaped behind some bushes.

"What is it?" asked Morgan.

"A walk-in interface with the ARKANE search engine. Once you've tried it, you'll want to spend all your research time there. You can see Martin's influences on the side."

Morgan grinned as she saw the little blue police box.

"Bigger on the inside, I guess?"

"Exactly." Jake explained further. "It's a virtual reality library where you can interact with the data in three dimensional space. In fact, it's modeled after the Bodleian Library in Oxford, so you'll feel right at home."

Morgan looked at the device. One of the reasons she had come to ARKANE was their mind-blowing access to knowledge. They gathered it from all corners of the earth and all faiths, hacked it from hidden archives and foreign intelligences and scanned it from ancient manuscripts. The data was bound together into a database that made Google look like an abacus. The possibilities were intoxicating to her. Jake seemed to regard knowledge as a tool for the blunt instrument of action but she saw it as a portal to understanding psychology and its link to the faith of the human race. Perhaps it was a key to finding her own path to God.

Jake walked back towards the door.

"Right, let's drop in on Martin and then we're off to see the Director. I know how much you're looking forward to that."

Morgan stuck her tongue out at him. It seemed their cheeky relationship was back on track.

Martin Klein's office was at the end of the long lab corridor, a little space that few were allowed to enter without an appointment. Jake knocked on the closed door which bore the nameplate 'Head Librarian.'

"He's way more than that, of course. He's the Brain of the Institute, but he likes the name." Jake said as the door opened.

"Jake, come in, come in." A tall man with roughly cut blond hair and thin wire-rimmed glasses beckoned them in. He bobbed up and down on the balls of his feet. "And welcome Dr Sierra."

He reached out his hand but then snatched it back before Morgan could take it. He spun round to his desk, speaking quickly, his mind jumping ahead.

"I have something here for you, I've been saving it. It's a paper on the meaning of the drawings in the Red Book and how they relate to the Jungian archetypes. I thought you would like it."

Morgan smiled and took the paper he held out. She knew a number of men and a few women who came under the high functioning Asperger's type and understood the avoidance of physical touch as well as the phenomenal mind that too many underestimated.

"Thank you Martin. That's very kind."

"And I have a new tablet for you, fully loaded with all the information you need to get started, an orientation of the pod system - that's the virtual library - as well as all the material I have so far on the Thanatos group, and of course the latest bombings and the prophecies and … "

Jake cut in.

"You're marvelous, Spooky. You know how much we appreciate your help. Morgan has to settle in today and we need to see Marietti, but we wanted to pick your brain first."

Jake's voice was soft and although Morgan could see he needed to guide Martin's enthusiasm sometimes, she could feel it was with real respect and friendship. Jake had told her that the 'Spooky' nickname came from Martin's uncanny ability to find patterns and answers in a mass of data. He could perceive hidden truths in the chaotic material he scanned that others would never see. Martin rocked back and forth on his heels for a moment, then picked up a colored marker and went to the back wall.

"Of course Jake, what do you need?"

"We have some disparate pieces of information that we somehow need to knit together," Jake replied. "Are they related, and if so, how? And are we dealing with Thanatos only or some other organization?"

Martin began to draw as Jake spoke, strange creatures with fantastical limbs surrounded by creepers and flowers. It was as if his creative brain needed to be occupied while he processed the incoming information with his logical side. Morgan was fascinated by how he could manipulate his mind in such a manner and she joined in the conversation.

"The suicides in Israel relate to the Revelation prophecy," she said. "The pale horse also links it to Thanatos, as they used the image in the hunt for the Pentecost stones. The prophecy says a quarter of the world must die. I think that's a threat we need to take seriously."

"But how could they possibly do it?" Jake asked.

"If I wanted to kill a quarter of the world," Martin mused, "then I would need something more than a few religious fanatics in Israel committing suicide. It's not a very good plan, is it?"

Morgan laughed.

"Good point. There must be something bigger going on. Perhaps this is just the beginning, but where is it heading?"

Jake paced the small office as he thought. Morgan knew

that he wanted to discover who was behind Thanatos as much as she did. Their clashes with members of the organization during the Pentecost operation had left scars on them both.

"Actually, that's a good way to think about it," Jake said. "If you were trying to destroy a quarter of the world, what would you do?"

"I'd release some kind of virus," said Martin. "But I'd also want to make sure the right people would survive before I started the mass destruction." He paused in his drawings. "Goodness, did I just say that? It sounds like eugenics, but I guess all the dictators in history have tried to do the same thing. You want to destroy the perceived 'Other' and protect the people you consider to be the right type of people to survive."

"That is exactly what I've seen in Africa," Jake replied, anger in his tawny eyes. "Look at Rwanda, the Congo. I know my own people in South Africa would have done that if they could. Apartheid was just one step from annihilation of the Other. I don't want to see that situation happen again."

"Eugenics isn't all bad." Martin adjusted his glasses. "I'm sorry Jake, but it seems that the perfectly reasonable science behind eugenics has been lost in all the bad press."

"Seriously?" Jake said. "Go on then, convince me."

Martin stood like a professor, bouncing with enthusiasm for his subject.

"Before Hitler, eugenics was considered a proper science, interested in researching how to make the overall population better. Of course, humanity has done this with animals and plants for generations, breeding for better stock or enhanced resistance to disease. Humans have had similar ideas, like marrying into a higher class and nowadays, women go to sperm banks and specifically choose a donor based on criteria that will make a better baby. There are designer genetics that screen for gender and disabilities, or the Tay Sachs register for Jews. All this is based on eugenics in the purest sense, which is about building better humans."

Jake raised an eyebrow.

Noticing his response, Morgan said, "He's right Jake. Tay Sachs is a genetic disease that manifests if both parents carry the gene so there is a screening program for Ashkenazi Jews. As a result it has been practically eliminated, as people are encouraged not to have children if they both have the gene." She turned. "But Martin, that's a positive example of education and personal choice to avoid future problems. We're talking here about the negative connotation of eugenics which is about destroying those who aren't considered worthy of life."

Martin flicked on a screen in front of him and accessed the powerful ARKANE search engine to highlight his points as he continued.

"Francis Galton was one of the great British polymaths of the nineteenth century and the Chair of Eugenics at University College, London. He was a statistician, an explorer, an inventor, an anthropologist and was also one of the early eugenicists, as well as being cousin to Charles Darwin."

The picture of Galton on the screen showed a stern man in a three piece suit, thin-lipped and heavy browed, his bald head tonsured with hair extending down into sideburns popular at the time.

"Galton had a phenomenal mind," Martin spoke rapidly, his words running together in his enthusiasm. "He applied statistical methods to the study of human difference. He devised the first weather map, discovered standard deviation, regression to the mean and crowd-sourcing … "

Jake interrupted again. "OK, so we get he was incredibly intelligent, but what has this got to do with eugenics?"

Martin adjusted his glasses.

"After Darwin published 'On the Origin of Species,' Galton devoted himself to investigating differences among humans. He traced great men through generations to see where their unusual abilities dropped away. It was Galton who actually coined the term 'eugenics.' At the peak of its popularity, it was supported by politicians like Winston Churchill and Roosevelt as well as great thinkers such as HG Wells and George Bernard Shaw."

"These are all men," Morgan noted, "but I can see how women would also be interested in this. I mean, doesn't everyone want the best for their child, starting with superior genes?"

"Actually, one of the more infamous proponents of eugenics was Marie Stopes," Martin replied.

"The campaigner for women's rights and birth control? Isn't the organization she founded still active today." Morgan said.

"Indeed. It's actually one of the UK's leading providers of sexual and reproductive healthcare services, and of course does an amazing job. But looking back at the founder, you might be surprised at what she believed."

Martin tapped his screen and it changed to show a black and white picture of a woman seated at a laboratory bench, microscope in front of her. Her hair was piled up on top of her head, wisps flying out.

"Stopes called for compulsory sterilization of those unfit for parenthood," Martin continued. "When her son married a short-sighted woman, she cut him out of her will and after her death, a large amount of her money went to the Eugenics Society, now called the Galton Institute for obvious reasons."

Jake was still puzzled.

"So some upper class Brits liked the idea of eugenics because they didn't want more useless mouths to feed. But that doesn't make it something that was accepted everywhere, does it?"

Martin shook his head.

"Incorrect Jake. It was huge in America, which is where

Hitler got his ideas from. The original sterilization of 'unfit' people started in the USA, with over 64,000 people sterilized by the various states. The Nazis used this example as justification of their own sterilization regime and this was expanded into the ideas of racial purity that still persist today."

"But eugenics was never supposed to be the basis for genocide," Morgan said. "It's important to remember that. In America and Britain, it didn't turn into killing those considered unfit, merely that they shouldn't have children."

"And how does eugenics relate to our current investigation?" Jake asked, frustration evident in his voice.

"I agree with Martin that it makes sense if there are two prongs to the fulfillment of the prophecy," Morgan replied. "If a quarter of the world must die, then who are they, and who will be saved? For that scale of attack there needs to be a huge plan in place and the prophecy mentions sword, famine, plague and wild beasts, so there's quite a scope of options to carry it out."

"As I said, plague would be easiest," Martin replied. "There's plenty of nasty viruses around."

Morgan paced as she spoke.

"Hmm, yes, perhaps, but there is a theological motivation behind this so I would suspect something less biological and more religious in nature. For example, why were Thanatos interested in the Pentecost stones?"

"Think about it," replied Jake. "If you wanted to ensure some people died and others lived, the Pentecost stones were evidence of a way to resurrect, to heal as well as to destroy. But they've clearly moved onto other things now."

His phone began to buzz. He ignored it.

"Racial targeting or religious destruction was exactly what Hitler aimed to do to the Jews. My father and I would have been included in the destruction," Morgan noted.

Martin sat down, taking off his glasses and rubbing his eyes.

"Me too. I'm considered defective, not worth breeding into the next generation. People like me would have also been destroyed."

Martin's phone buzzed next. He also ignored it, engrossed in the discussion.

"So, we can see the arguments for this in a truly ideological sense," Morgan continued. "I mean we would all improve the human race if we could, but it can't be done without gross violation of human rights. Thanatos seems to be emerging as a self-appointed God-like organization deciding who deserves to live or die. So how might this be done, and how can we stop it?"

The desk phone started to ring and the 'Jaws' suspense music filled the room. Martin grimaced.

"That's Marietti. Guess it's urgent. Something must have happened."

CHAPTER 13

THE DOOR TO THE anteroom opened and Maria looked up. Armen Harghada walked in, and brought with him an atmosphere of regret that sank her heart. His face was set in a mask but she knew he was never sent to talk to successful funding candidates. Even as he stood in the doorway, she was already calculating what she could do next to salvage her research, perhaps take it to another institute.

"Dr Van Garre, if you would please follow me. There are some matters we need to attend to."

She stood and walked to the door. Maria felt desperate but Harghada still held the ear of Milan Noble. What if she could convince him of the need to continue the research?

"Perhaps I could show you the research personally, sir?"

Harghada paused. "I think that might be a good idea. How long did you say the results take to manifest?"

"With the highest pulse frequencies and some suscepti-bility to obedience, we can see an effect in as little as one session," she replied, trying to hide the hope in her voice. "Certain drugs increase susceptibility."

They entered the elevator and she noticed as he swiped his card that there were levels she had never seen before that looked to be below ground. He caught her attention.

"There are more wonders here at Zoebios than you could ever imagine," he said, but Maria thought his smile was hollow, and his eyes belonged to a man who had seen haunting things. No matter, Maria knew he could still save her research and so she would turn on the charm and prove her research had potential.

They walked into the lab and the groups of people waiting for news melted back into their work at Maria's stony gaze. She showed Harghada to her office.

"Perhaps you would close the lab for the rest of the day," he said, "and we could examine your research together in private. Is that to your satisfaction?"

The question was rhetorical of course. She felt his penetrating gaze on her back as she went to tell her staff to take a well-earned afternoon off. The lab cleared out fast, and Maria returned to her office to find Harghada gazing at the Escher print.

"How true this is," he said. "I think perhaps the Zoebios emblem should be replaced by something like this. It more accurately reflects our path in the world, for it takes death for new life, and darkness for the light to stand out." He turned to face her. "Now Doctor, convince me not to shut this lab down."

"Of course. I've prepared some videos so you can witness the response of subjects under the treatment regime. If you would sit here, I'll talk you through them."

Harghada spun round, his eyes narrowing. "I've seen all your facts and figures and it's not enough. At this point I need more practical evidence. Show me how it works with you as the subject."

Maria frowned. Of course she had tried the equipment herself, at a mild dosage in order to experience some of the effects, but never without supervision. "It could be dangerous. I would need one of my team to assist."

Harghada shook his head.

"I'm afraid not. I shall be your assistant. If you want to convince me to keep the lab open, then this is your only chance."

Maria considered how to proceed. It could be done as long as he followed her directions. After all, she believed in her research, and what harm could come to her in her own lab?

"OK," she nodded warily. "The treatment room is at the back of the lab."

She led him through the now empty floor, past the evidence of a busy lab suspended for the day. She pointed at a row of booths at the back of a side-room. There was a bed in each, with a pair of enlarged earphones lying on the blanket. Syringes and other medical equipment lay in sterilized pouches at the side of the room.

"What has been your most effective case so far?" Harghada asked.

Maria suddenly realized what he would ask her to do. Could she lie to him now? But he had already seen the results in the presentation and he was leading her into a trap of her own making. Her heart pounded as she considered her options.

"Come on Doctor, surely you know your own results," he said, goading her. "You have had other people under your care. Would you not subject yourself to the same situation? I'm a medical doctor, so I can assist with whatever you need. I have a meeting with Milan later and your own test results would go a long way to deciding what happens next with this research."

Maria took a deep breath. All her instincts said she should not give this man power over her but she couldn't walk away from this last chance.

"Fine, but I need to show you how it all works before I go under." She walked ahead of him into a glass-walled area. "This is where we record the suggestions to go under the binaural beats. They are fed into the headphones you can see on the beds. They're modified to stimulate the temporal lobe so the commands are paired with the perception of the Other."

Harghada leaned in to look more closely at the recording unit.

"I'd like to make a new recording without you knowing what I'm saying. That way I can be sure that you aren't faking your response."

"I don't think that would be ethical or practical," said Maria, a little panicked now. "Perhaps this was a bad idea."

She turned to walk out of the booth. He grabbed her wrist and twisted her back towards him, his grip tight but controlled, as if he could snap her wrist if he applied just a little more pressure.

"Dr Van Garre," Harghada purred, a cat playing with its prey. "Now is not the time to be coy about your research. You will show me how this works." He let her go, his voice cajoling. "Trust me. I just want to see if you were telling the truth this morning. Prove it and I will be the strongest advocate for your work, personally guaranteeing your funding."

Maria was shaking now. If she ran for the door, she knew he would stop her. His eyes were feral, a wolf whose jaws were itching to clamp down on her soft flesh. She bit her lip, willing herself to stay in control, and pointed at the controls.

"It's quite easy. We'll use booth one, so you click the button for 1, record the message and click it again. The message will be repeated under the binaural beat rhythm at different levels. The subject needs to be guided in slowly, as the highest frequency is too much straight away, but that's controlled automatically by the program."

Harghada nodded.

"Go and lie down while I do the recording." She started to walk out. "And don't try anything, Doctor. It would always be your word against mine in this building. Just be a good girl, and let's do this experiment together."

Maria smarted at his words but, feeling like she had no choice, she walked back into the booth area and lay down on the bed. She pulled her pinstriped suit jacket closer around her, trying to warm her body against the chill of fear. She could see Harghada recording something, his fleshy lips moving silently behind the glass. She pulled on the headset and waited, wondering what he was saying, fearful of the thoughts that would enter her subconscious. But then he came out of the booth.

"I think you've forgotten something."

Maria sat up again.

"No, that's all you need to do for the audio channel."

"I clearly recall you mentioning that the best results were binaural beats paired with a drug regime." He walked to the table of syringes, his fingers running over the sealed packets. Maria felt the blood leave her face. "You said the effects were enhanced with a hallucinogen," Harghada continued. "If we're trying to give you visions of God, then we'd better make the experience worthwhile. I bet you have some LSD somewhere, since your research is influenced by Aldous Huxley."

"Huxley voluntarily took drugs, and I will not." Maria stood up and faced Harghada, shaking with anger and indignation. "I will sacrifice my research but not my safety and I'm leaving now. I don't believe you ever intended to consider this for further funding. I don't know what you're doing but I won't be part of it."

She tried to push past him but he grabbed her arm. She struggled and he pushed her towards the bed, backhanding her so she fell, clutching her stinging face.

"How dare you touch me?" Maria shouted.

Harghada laughed.

"You are nothing Doctor. Remember that. Now, I want to

get on with this experiment and you will be my subject."

Maria ran for the door. He caught her and hit her again with an open hand. He forced her back to the bed and pressed her face down into the pillow until she stopped screaming. Her struggles grew weaker. He let her go on the edge of unconsciousness and she gasped for breath, struggling to draw air into her lungs. Weakened, she felt him tie her hands and feet to the bed. He stuffed a sterile dressing into her mouth.

"That will keep you quiet. Now, where is that LSD?"

Maria watched in horror as he rifled through the drug cabinet. She was desperate to stop him but unable to move. She moaned against the gag, fighting against the bonds.

"Here it is. I knew you'd be arrogant enough to keep some. Hard to resist the inexplicable, isn't it."

He filled a syringe and advanced on her.

"Just relax, Doctor. This is the culmination of your research after all. You will finally get to experience the rush. You will see God."

He pushed the needle into her arm and she began to feel its effects almost immediately. He put the headset over her ears again. Her fear sank away as the colors in the room grew more intense. Out of the corner of her eye, she watched him go to the booth and switch on the machine. She heard rushing in her ears, a waterfall of sound and she relaxed into the noise. Her eyes closed involuntarily and she began to sense a Being in the room with her, a presence that calmed and soothed. Her scientist's mind was still a little alert and part of her knew this was the effect of the stimulation of her temporal lobe, the interaction of the drug and the binaural suggestion. But a primal part of her just wanted to be lost in the experience. The Being was speaking now, commanding and she had to obey. Was this how the others felt as they slipped under? The waterfall grew louder and her own thoughts were lost in the rush.

Harghada watched as Maria twitched and then went still, her face transfigured with wonder. A part of him was desperate to see these visions for himself, but then he didn't believe in any kind of God. However, it would be interesting to know what he would see under the spell of the beats. Would it be the demons of hell or just an expanse of emptiness?

He untied Maria from the bed and took the makeshift gag from her mouth. She would be no trouble now, not if her research was truly as transformative as she believed. He touched the gun in its holster under his arm. If this didn't work, there were other ways of dealing with her but he needed to have proof to show Milan for the next phase. Would the suggestion he planted take hold? If it did, they could release her research with the knowledge that destruction could be taken to the masses.

Maria suddenly sat up on the bed and he stepped away from her, giving her space. Her eyes were open but staring past him, her mouth moving in a trance-like mantra. She removed the headphones and stood, her prayers only whispers now, the words all jumbled together. But she was smiling, a beatific vision transforming her face to that of a much younger woman.

Harghada followed her out of the treatment room and back to her office where Maria knelt by the large picture window, rocking backwards and forwards in worship. He stood behind her, his gun ready in case she came out of the trance. Her words ran together, faster and faster as she rocked, and then suddenly she stopped. She was silent and still for a moment, and then she spoke clearly.

"I will obey."

Her words shocked Harghada, even though it was as she had promised. He watched as she lifted a heavy paperweight from her desk, a chunk of vermilion crystal, and threw it at the large glass window. It bounced off the safety glass. She picked it up again and went to the window, banging it over and over again.

"I. Will. Obey," she said between smashes onto the glass. Harghada could see it would take time to get through the glass with that rock and she would exhaust herself. What if she came out of the trance in the meantime? He made a decision and slipped the gun into her other hand and then retreated around the far side of the desk. Her fingers tightened as she seemed to realize what she held. For a moment, Harghada thought he had made a terrible mistake, as she raised the gun in his direction.

At the last moment, she swung round and shot double-tap into the window, which splintered and cracked. She shot again, emptying the gun and a large hole was blown out into the grey Paris sky. From the twenty-first floor, there were views all the way to the Seine. Harghada pulled the security alarm for the sake of appearance, for it had to look as if he had tried to stop her. Maria stepped over the glass to the window, dropped the gun and just walked out. No final words, no look back, no hesitation. Harghada was amazed at the result, for the research truly worked and Milan was going to love the elegant solution. The wind whistled in through the gap as the security team burst through from the main stairwell. Harghada smiled inwardly. The delivery mechanism worked, now they just needed the message.

CHAPTER 14

ELIAS MARIETTI RESTED HIS head in his hands, fingers massaging his temples as another starburst of pain rocketed through his brain. The call from the Vatican had set off a migraine that had been lurking in the background for days, waiting for him to lower his guard. The Devil's Bible was under threat and the Cardinal had been adamant that they must locate and secure it before dark forces could wield its power. How he longed to go back out in the field himself instead of being stuck here in the public offices of ARKANE. He looked out of the tall window towards Trafalgar Square. He felt like one of the great lions trapped in bronze at the base of Nelson's Column, old fighters reined in to provide an illusion of strength to the Empire. It felt as if the days were getting shorter and time was speeding up. Events were escalating throughout the globe and he could feel the vibrations of those who sought to remove him from this position. He knew too much, and yet they couldn't act, because they knew what he could do to them.

Marietti thought back to when he had been young, so focused on what he could achieve for the glory of God and the Church. Over time he had become disillusioned with the way the Church hid the secrets that he investigated. Of course, if people knew that supernatural happenings were so commonplace, how would the Church keep so much power? If people knew the secrets he kept, why would they blindly follow a tradition that encouraged middlemen between individuals and the world of consciousness that awaited them. Marietti felt the pull of the secrets that lay down in the Vaults. Some called to him in the night, their power earthed in the protected tomb. I must ask Martin to add further precautions to the access sequence, he thought, for I will need protection from myself soon enough.

He looked up at the painting newly installed in his office and for a moment lost himself in its depths. It was Salvador Dali's Christ of St John of the Cross, a painting he had coveted for many years and had finally managed to borrow for a time. It depicted the crucified Jesus suspended above a lake dotted with fishermen, a swirling cloudy sky and gusts whipping across the waters. The perspective looked down from the top of Christ's head giving the viewer a sense of being in space, as if God looked down over quiet waters. It was also a bloodless crucifixion, with no instruments of torture to be seen. Marietti found a transient peace in the image, as if all was right with heaven. Although he felt supernatural forces arrayed on both sides, for a moment, there was stillness and he considered it a perk of the job to be able to have such magnificent paintings in his sanctuary.

There was a knock at the door.

"Enter," he called, snapping himself back into officious mode as Jake Timber and Morgan Sierra stepped through the door, summoned by his urgent calls. He stood to greet them.

"Welcome Morgan, I'm so glad you've decided to join us." Marietti extended his hand. Her handshake was firm and she met his eyes with an unflinching gaze.

"Thank you, Director. I'm looking forward to starting work on this new case."

"Jake."

"Sir."

The men acknowledged each other with an easy familiarity.

"That's a Dali," Morgan said. She raised an eyebrow, clearly impressed with the Director's choice of artwork.

"On loan for only a few weeks before it's returned to Glasgow."

"It's gorgeous."

Marietti smiled. He could see her wondering what other treasures he had.

"I know you'll enjoy working here, Morgan. Now, to business. Cardinal Brazza called from the Vatican. The Capela dos Ossos in Evora, Portugal has been ransacked and one of the priests tortured and murdered."

"What was taken?" Jake asked.

"Nothing," Marietti replied. "That's the problem. We think they're after the Devil's Bible, and if so, I'm certain Thanatos is behind it."

Morgan looked confused. "I thought the Devil's Bible was held at the National Library in Sweden."

"That's where you should think it is, but the Capela was only one of its other rumored resting places," Marietti picked up his tablet computer and flicked to the ARKANE search engine, calling up the records for the Devil's Bible. The screen on the wall came alive with the image of a huge book bound with wooden boards and metal clasps.

"It's the biggest medieval manuscript in the world, also known as the Codas Gigas," Marietti explained. "Its real power lies in the words within. The legend behind it says that a monk broke his vows and was sentenced to be walled up alive. To save himself, he promised that he would complete a book containing all human knowledge in just one night. In the early hours of the morning, when it became clear he could not complete the task, he called on Lucifer to help him in exchange for his soul. When the abbot came the next morning, the book was finished, but along with the Biblical verses were inscribed curses, spells and images of demonic figures."

"Why would Thanatos want it?" Jake asked. "And what's this got to do with the prophecy?"

Marietti sighed. The sins of the fathers revisited on this generation indeed, he thought.

"The Devil's Bible in the Swedish library isn't the real one," he said, with a sigh. "It's a fake that has been used to keep the real secrets of the Bible from scholars and the inevitable crazies who flock to see it. If you know where to look, the trail points to the Capela dos Ossos as the real hiding place, but it's not there either."

"So what's in the authentic Devil's Bible to make someone want it so much?" Morgan asked, leaning forward in her seat. Marietti flicked the tablet screen and entered his password to access the secret archives of the ARKANE database. The image that came onto the screen was a beautifully rendered illustration of the pale horse of the apocalypse rearing up, its rider a hooded skeleton. Under the horse's hooves were trampled bodies of the dead. Around the illustration were faint words but the scale meant they could not be made out.

"The pale horse again," Jake said. "But what's the big deal? What power can words from an ancient manuscript have in the twenty-first century?"

Marietti stood and walked towards the Dali painting.

"The power of these words cannot be underestimated Jake. When the Devil's Bible was rediscovered in the Czech Republic it was taken to the Vatican. During the investigation, the words from these pages were spoken aloud."

"What happened?" Morgan asked.

"We only know the aftermath, but it is written that the monk who read the words tore apart his colleagues with bare hands and teeth. It was as if he was possessed with an incredible strength and a lust for blood. He became the wild beast of the prophecy and the bodies of the others were as this image, trampled underfoot as if by rampaging horses."

Jake shook his head.

"You're saying that this is some kind of curse? That the speaker goes berserk in the classic sense of the warrior crazed with bloodlust in the heat of battle? I've seen some crazy things but - "

"What happened to the Bible after that?" Morgan asked, cutting off Jake's tirade.

"A careful copy was made, omitting the final pages and also the curses written throughout the book. Other, more simple phrases were included about exorcism and demons, enough to keep people interested but nothing that could harm anyone. The faintly comical painting of the Devil was added as a way to ensure the book stayed known as the Devil's Bible and the Vatican hid the real book deep in its archives, an uncategorized manuscript amongst thousands of others. Only a few men knew of it, those who could be trusted to keep it hidden."

"So what triggered the attack in Portugal?" Jake asked.

"During the dark days of the Second World War, the Vatican contained some who were sympathetic to the Nazi cause and Hitler had a team dedicated to seeking powerful occult objects. The Devil's Bible was on their list, although even they didn't know what it truly represented. The Vatican vaults were considered too dangerous for many of the objects at that time and the most powerful were smuggled out. We have some here in the crypt, but the Devil's Bible was taken to a secret location. Official records say it lies at the Capela dos Ossos so clearly someone has accessed those records and wants the Bible." Marietti paced the room, his face lined with worry. "Truly this object has terrifying power, whether you believe it could be real or not. I know of men who were changed by those events and wrote personal accounts of their experiences. They understood the power of evil and spent the rest of their lives on their knees every night asking for deliverance. I trust the words they wrote were truth, so you must retrieve the Devil's Bible. It isn't safe out there. We must bring it back immediately."

"So where is it?" asked Jake. "We'll go at once."

Marietti paused. The weight of long years of silence pressed down upon him. To speak the location now would mean that the Devil's Bible would be out in the open again, a danger to all, but he had no choice. Finally he spoke.

"It's at the Capuchin monastery in Palermo, a fitting place to consider the death that awaits us all."

"Why? What's there?" Jake asked.

"You need to go and see for yourself," Marietti replied. "I've told the Abbot you're coming for research purposes. He doesn't know about the book, none of them do, although many rumors have surfaced over the years. I don't know where it is within the crypt. You'll need to figure that out." He looked at Morgan. "I'm concerned for what could be done with this book. It was never fully studied, never investigated further because of that incident."

"Why wasn't it destroyed?" she asked, "if it was that dangerous?"

Marietti shook his head, recalling the mistakes of his own past.

"The fatal flaw of those that seek spiritual truth is that they cannot destroy even that which is truly evil," he said. "The book still contains the holy word of God as well as curses, so it could not be burnt. But I'm afraid of what could happen if the knowledge of what it can do was known by others. If Thanatos find it first it could be the trigger for an escalation of their plans."

"We'll go as soon as we can get the team together," Jake said as he stood to leave.

"No team, just you two. Get in and out quickly and quietly. Keep this low profile and top secret." Marietti swiped at the screen, tapping with his fingertip.

"There, I've opened the Devil's Bible file for you in the archives. You won't be able to read the inscriptions, they were all scrubbed from the images in case someone accessed it by mistake. But it should give you somewhere to start, and something to read on your journey."

Marietti waved them out and turned back to the Dali painting. The lake below Christ was deceptively calm but there was a storm brewing in the distance, bringing chaos and destruction in its wake.

CHAPTER 15

Catacombe dei Cappucini, Palermo, Sicily. 9.07pm

"So you're saying that the monastery crypt is full of dead bodies?" asked Jake as their taxi sped from the airport towards the Capuchin monastery. "That's normal though, right?"

"Yes, but these are clothed and more like mummies than skeletons. They still look like people," Morgan replied.

"That just seems weird. Shame we have to go in after dark."

Morgan laughed.

"You big baby. It wasn't so long ago we were creeping round Venice after midnight."

"Yes, but there weren't any zombie looking bodies there. I prefer my dead people completely dead."

Jake returned to studying the Devil's Bible file as if he could solve the puzzle of its location by looking harder at it. Morgan gazed out of the window at the city speeding by as memories of that night in Venice replayed in her mind. They had spoken of faith and God in the darkness of the ancient Basilica before the revelation of the Pentecost mural. She had surprised herself that night by sharing stories of her own spiritual experience, but then it had been a magical place and thing were different now. Then she was fighting to save her sister and niece, now she was Jake's partner at ARKANE, although how well their partnership would work still remained to be seen.

Glimpses of Palermo's architecture reminded Morgan that this ancient city had been founded by the Phoenicians nearly three thousand years ago and had been influenced by every major civilization since then. Even today it was an important port in southern Italy, famous for its gastronomy and architecture as much as for the Sicilian mafia.

The taxi pulled up outside the Capuchin catacombs. Jake paid the driver and went to talk to the lone security guard at the entrance. After a moment, he waved them through nonchalantly, clearly settling in for a quiet night listening to sport on the radio.

"He says the abbot is in the crypt and will give us the tour before he leaves for the night," Jake said, as Morgan joined him. They headed down into the crypt in an elevator, then walked down a long corridor at the lowest level which finally opened up into a large room.

Morgan looked around in fascination. The bodies exhibited here were fully dressed, some just skulls and others with brown skin stretched around screaming heads like mummified horrors. The bodies were stacked two levels high, hung on hooks to keep them stable in a minstrel's gallery of mortality. Their clothes were mainly in tatters now, but Morgan could see that they had once been fine fabrics with trimmings of lace and fur. She looked more closely at one of the mummies. His teeth were bared in a grimace, lips shrunken back, eyelashes still lay upon leathery cheeks. He had been posed as if at prayer, in a tribute to the God he expected to meet in the hereafter.

"Benvenuti," a voice said. Morgan and Jake both started, snapped out of their fascinated contemplation. "Scusi, scusi, I didn't meant to make you jump. I'm Abbot Scorienza. Welcome to the crypt." The abbot stepped towards them, pulling back the cowl that hid his face. He was an eerie exten-sion of the place, skin tight around his face, his bald head reflecting the dim lights. "You must be from ARKANE. You certainly keep some odd hours for research but, for sure, it's more peaceful down here at night. We have a lot of tourists in the daytime. The face of death has many admirers."

"This is an amazing place," Morgan said, a friendly smile on her face. It would be helpful to have the abbot onside. "Please tell us more about it. These people are clearly not all monks."

"True, true. The Capuchin monastery outgrew its original cemetery in the sixteenth century. The monks started bring-ing bodies down here and found that mysterious natural chemicals helped mummify them. It became popular with local aristocrats to have your body placed down here after death, dressed up for the occasion. People would visit the bodies and even change their clothes. If the families contin-ued to pay, the body would stay in these upright galleries. If they stopped paying, they would be lain in the racks." He pointed to a series of wooden racks, macabre bunk-beds with bodies stacked in them. Morgan noticed one with a rusty crown lying on an embroidered pillow, a hint of scarlet still in the robes he wore.

The Abbot led them on through more corridors and Morgan sneezed as the dust of old corpses swirled around them.

"How many bodies are down here?" Jake asked.

"Around eight thousand. We have separated them into galleries for men, women, children, virgins, priests, monks and professors. We even have the great painter Velasquez."

"You have children here too?" Morgan said. "That must be so sad."

"You can see for yourself," the Abbot replied as they turned a corner into a hall with alcoves on the wall and caskets on the floor. Jake walked ahead into the room. She saw him cross himself as he walked to an open casket and looked down at a tiny skeleton still dressed in a christening robe. He bent to look more closely at the tiny body, its skeletal head turned to one side, bony thumb angled towards where the baby mouth would have been. A familiar sadness welled up inside Morgan as she thought of Elian, and of her parents. Elian had been snatched away too soon and thoughts of the children they might have had together glimmered in her mind. Death wasn't a stranger to her. She had fought against him before and although she would keep fighting, she knew that he would eventually win, but not just yet. She turned back to the Abbot.

"Do any of the bodies have books or possessions with them?" she asked.

Jake looked around expectantly.

"There are some." The abbot shrugged. "But not so many. Why? Is that what you're looking for?"

"We just have some fact checking to do," Jake said, dodging the question. "Thank you for your help. We'll need a few hours down here if that's OK?"

"Si figuri, don't mention it." The Abbot turned to leave. "You can stay down here as long as you want. I find it a peaceful place. After all, we don't have to be afraid of the dead for they are in glory. Buonanotte. Goodnight."

He walked away down the corridor and was soon lost in the gloom, his brown habit blending with the deep shadows.

"Are you alright?" Morgan asked Jake. His eyes were sepia in this half-light, the spark she usually saw dulled with memory. She reached out to touch his arm gently.

"These bodies. These babies." He turned away from her. "I was in Rwanda."

The word was enough for her to understand his emotion. It conjured images of mass graves, almost one million people massacred, even children hacked to pieces.

"I can cope with the death of grown men and women, but not children. But these little ones are so peaceful, I don't even know why it sparked the memory. It's such a different place to that desperate time."

"Perhaps this proximity to death allows you to feel and express what's usually buried," Morgan questioned. "Perhaps it's cathartic."

"OK, that's quite enough deep and meaningful discussion," Jake said. "Let's find this diabolical book and get out of here. This atmosphere is just a little too intense for the middle of the night. So where do we start?" He looked at Morgan. "You're the psychologist. Where would you put the Devil's Bible if you were trying to hide it from evil Vatican Nazi spies?"

She laughed at his hyperbole, the serious atmosphere broken.

"I'd want to hide it but I'd also want to protect it somehow. Maybe behind some kind of altar, in the hope that prayer and faith would somehow negate its energy? There are also a number of closed caskets here according to the files. We would need to check the dates on those as the Devil's Bible was moved in the 1940s and the last mummy was put down here in 1920."

Together they walked back along the arm of the corridor towards the main entrance hall, ready to begin the search. Their footsteps echoed through the halls, muted by the cadaverous army hanging alongside them. Thin fluorescent tubes flickered overhead as if the old electric circuits were about to give out.

"Do you believe that the curses in the Devil's Bible could work?" Jake asked. "I've never seen Marietti look so scared but it just seems crazy to think mere words could turn someone into a demonic mass murderer."

Morgan considered for a moment, then spoke with hesitation.

123

"The spoken word has always been considered powerful in religion. God said 'let there be light' and there was light. He spoke again and created the world and humanity. Then of course the Bible says that the Word of God became flesh, perhaps the ultimate example of power. In occult practices and witchcraft, the spoken word in the form of curses is what actually brings forth demonic power. To speak something into the world with intent is somehow to create it, to make it real. That's why prayer is often spoken aloud, why converting to a faith must be professed with speech and not just in the mind."

"Which all sounds reasonable, but turning a monk into a crazed killer with one recitation of some kind of curse. Is that even possible?"

Morgan nodded. "There are documented cases where people have died because they believed they were cursed. Such is the power of words combined with belief."

"You're avoiding the question, but personally, I won't be reading anything from any book we find." Jake grinned at her. "OK, you search down that wing and I'll take this one. I want to get out of here as soon as possible."

"Likewise," Morgan said.

She turned down the corridor towards the women's section, the white vaulted ceiling arching above her. The mummies here wore dresses with bonnets and ribbons, although the material sagged around missing torsos padded with straw. Some mummies wore gloves as if they were about to take tea and two skeletons bent their heads together as if gossiping. Virgins were distinguished with metal bands around their heads, sainted with haloes in death. Morgan looked around carefully. Each mummy stood in an alcove in the wall. There wasn't space to hide a book there. Equally the wooden stacks of bodies weren't deep enough to conceal the huge Codas Gigas. Morgan had read that the monastery had been bombed during the Second World War, after the book had been hidden here. There had also been a fire in 1966. Somehow the book must have escaped notice all that time so it must be well hidden. She scanned the caskets stacked on shelves above the bodies but all were too slim to contain the volume.

At the end of the corridor she spotted a simple altar. It was a long rectangle, certainly deep enough for a book to be hidden inside. With anticipation, Morgan walked over and lifted the altarpiece. Dust rose into the air and she coughed, horribly aware of what she was breathing. Pulling the drapes back gingerly, Morgan could see that the altar was just a rough wooden box set on the stone floor. It didn't seem to be attached in any way. She knelt down and crawled around it looking for any way through the wood or for a chink to see inside. She could feel the cold, hard flagstones through her jeans and she shivered, and not just with the temperature. This place was beginning to get to her, for there were echoes of the past hiding here in dark corners, nightmares of little children locked below, their flesh decomposing over centuries. Perhaps it was unnatural, the way the physical bodies had remained so long after the soul had departed. It felt like Death's trophy case, with bodies stolen from a world of light and life above.

Morgan shook her head. Enough morbid contemplation, she thought. She continued to feel her way around the edge of the wood until she found a little door behind the altar. It had a plaque with an inscription dated 1947. Morgan's heart leapt. Perhaps this was the right place. The door was too small to push the Codas Gigas through but it could have been kept under here. She pulled at the tiny door. No movement. She slipped off her pack, dug out her penknife and levered the door, rattling it. The old lock broke and the door popped open. Morgan shone her torch into the space beyond. All she could see were piles of dusty prayer books, none of which could be the Codas Gigas as they were too small. It definitely wasn't here.

Suddenly a gunshot sounded in the dark hallway behind her, echoing off the high vaulted ceilings. Instinctively, Morgan crouched low behind the altar but the sound was further away and she realized quickly that she wasn't in immediate danger. Jake, she thought, her heart racing. Pulling her weapon from the shoulder holster, Morgan ran on light feet towards the sound, as silent mummies looked down on her with vacant eyes.

Jake had dived behind a huge casket a moment before the shot came, alerted by a slight stumbling step. The bullet thunked into the hard wood of the ancient coffin, splintering it but not passing through. He pulled his gun and returned fire, a double-tap in the direction the bullet had come from. It might keep them back for a few moments, he thought, willing Morgan to return as backup. Then he saw the grenade rolling across the floor towards him. No time to stop it. There was a stone sarcophagus on the other side of the room. Jake commando-rolled over and threw himself behind it as the grenade exploded and the world went black.

Morgan tried to stay silent as she ran towards the gunfire but with the explosion she gave up and just ran as fast as she could, weapon drawn. If Jake was pinned down, she had to get to him. She reached the entrance to the children's corridor where Jake had been searching. It had seemed a small explosion but the bodies were shredded from the walls and smoke billowed from the inner crypt. Tatters of cloth fluttered down in the carnage and ravaged skeletons lay broken on the stone paving. It was a massacre of the already dead, their bodies submitted to a final reckoning, but there was no sign of the living. Where was Jake?

She was too late to catch who had done this. The perpetrators must have left immediately and her thoughts flew to the Abbot and the security guard. Would they come running at the noise? Had the Thanatos team found them already? She had to find Jake.

The smoke cleared a little as it was sucked out by the ventilation system towards the main stairwell. Morgan held her sleeve over her mouth and nose and ducked down, crawling into the crypt. Her eyes pricked with tears from the smoke but there were no billowing flames. Clearly the grenade had been a mechanism to stun rather than aimed to kill, but she still couldn't see Jake and there was no human body amongst the mess of broken bones and ripped cloth on the floor. Then she spotted the sarcophagus, an ideal shield against the blast. It was where she would have hidden. She crawled below the smoke and saw Jake, his body wedged into the space between the wall and the stone.

"Jake, are you OK?" She shook his shoulder anxiously.

He groaned, eyelids flickering. There was a nasty slash wound on his head, a bruised bump swelling around it. It looked like some masonry had been dislodged and hit him in the blast. Blood trickled from the wound, highlighting his corkscrew scar. She pulled a sterile dressing from her pack and pressed it against his face, fingers lingering briefly on the puckered flesh as she added surgical tape to hold it in place. It would do for now. Jake was covered in slivers of bone and rags from the tattered clothing as well as fine masonry dust. Morgan almost gagged to think that they were now breathing in the bodies of these long dead children, powdered by the attack.

"I think you're concussed. I need to get you out of here,"

she said. With the smoke clearing, she was able to stand and assess how to move him. The rest of his body looked intact but with concussion he would be nauseous and dizzy. A big man, Jake was over six foot of muscle now crammed behind a stone mausoleum.

"I'm going to need your help partner," she said.

Jake groaned again, his eyes fluttering open. He put his hand against the wall, as if to anchor himself in the physical world.

"Did you get them?" he whispered, the effort causing him to wince with pain.

"No, by the time I arrived, there was no one else here. Now we need to get you out of here. You're going to have to shuffle back this way."

Jake pulled himself up.

"Lean forward," Morgan helped him around the end of the sarcophagus, appreciating the brief moment of being close to him. He coughed, a racking sound that echoed in the chamber. She passed him some water from her backpack. "How are you feeling now?"

Jake smiled with half-shut eyes.

"Like they blew me up, what do you think?"

His mocking tone reassured her. He wasn't too badly injured if he could still be so cocky, but he looked pale and ready to vomit at any point. Concussion could have other side effects and he needed to rest.

"We still need to find that book," Jake said. "Did you find anything?"

"Nothing and I don't even know where we should be looking," Morgan glanced around the ruined room. "We'd better get out of here soon because the explosion will have attracted attention. Perhaps the Abbot is hurt as well."

"It wasn't a professional attempt to kill me," Jake replied. "Perhaps more to dissuade us from our search. The shot was clumsy, and the grenade was old. I think we need to keep looking. Maybe we're closer than we think."

He blanched and Morgan could almost see the wave of pain rocket through him. He rubbed his head, fingers gently exploring the plastered wound. She turned away from his vulnerability, knowing she would want that courtesy from him and looked around the room. The little coffins were devastating in their size, many of them open caskets where tiny bodies now lay broken. One stood out as a newer addition to the vault and the explosion had ripped a large crack through the middle of it. It had a plaque on it, 'Rosalia Lombardo, 1920' and the glass top was covered in dust and debris.

Morgan used her forearm to swipe the fragments off the coffin and then gasped at the face within. For a moment she saw Gemma, her little niece, perfect face frozen in death. But then the vision cleared. It was a little girl, her skin a waxy orange-brown but still real skin. Her hair was caught back in a ponytail with an orange ribbon tied in a bow and curls were tangled on her forehead. Eyelashes lay upon perfect cheeks and a cupids' bow mouth gave the image of a sleeping beauty, innocence captured in a glass cage. She was wrapped in sienna silk, tucked in by the loving hands of a parent.

"Jake, come and look at this. She was laid to rest in 1920. That's the most recent burial and perhaps the one people would least notice changes to back in the 1940s."

Jake lurched over, using the remaining coffins as support. He looked down at the little girl.

"She seems to have beaten death at least in the physical sense," he said. "But it just doesn't make sense to me how these bodies can look so real. There's no life spark here, just a treated bag of skin and bones."

Morgan was startled by his vehemence and she realized that she didn't actually know that much about his past or what drove him in this work. There would be time for that later, she thought.

"The glass has been cracked by the explosion." Her

fingers probed a fracture in the smooth surface. "The air will destroy her perfect looks now. She'll soon be a ghoul like the rest of them."

Morgan followed the crack down the side of the coffin and into the base. It sat upon a dais of sorts and the explosion had dislodged it. She knelt for a better look.

"Give me a hand moving this," she said, the body of the little girl forgotten now, collateral damage in the hunt for something far more dangerous. Jake braced himself and groaned with the pain, but he helped her to lift the coffin from the top of the raised platform and place it gently on the floor. In a hollowed out compartment beneath lay a huge rectangular shape wrapped in sackcloth.

"That's got to be it," Morgan said, barely suppressed excitement in her voice. "Help me get it out of there."

Again they lifted together, Jake grimacing as he heaved. Blood dripped down the side of his face from under the dressing. The book weighed seventy five kilos and Morgan could see the strain was increasing the pain in his head as they dropped the huge parcel on the floor with a thump. Jake leant on the wall as Morgan knelt and pulled back the sackcloth to reveal the book. Its front cover was decorated in an ornate pattern that hadn't been clear on the images Marietti had shown them. Morgan stretched out her hand to open a clasp.

"Don't," Jake said, his words a sharp rebuke. She looked up at him.

"You seriously think there's something to these curses?" she asked.

Jake was silent. Morgan could see that he was wrestling with rationality that fought hard against his spiritual side but she felt an almost palpable energy emanating from the book. It wanted her to open it and she didn't want to resist. Taking Jake's silence as a kind of permission, she flicked open the clasps one by one and opened the book, hefting the large wooden cover so it lay on the floor.

Hi curiosity piqued now, Jake came to kneel unsteadily next to her and together they gazed at the intricate colors of the richly illuminated pages. The initials of the first word on every page were decorated with medieval images of saints and Biblical figures. Angels and demons roamed the margins, hunting each other through the forest of pages.

"It's beautiful," Morgan said.

"But deadly," Jake whispered, his voice lowered in the close air of the crypt.

"Marietti said the curses were at the back," Morgan turned the pages over carefully in larger chunks to get to the back of the book faster. She spoke the names of the books with familiarity, "Isaiah, Zephaniah, Romans, Hebrews. Here it is…Revelation. Oh, it's amazing."

The chapter began with the glorious vision of Christ coming on a cloud with the whole cosmos arrayed before him. The seven lamp-stands were illuminated in real gold leaf, the seven stars of heaven in silver and a sword stood from his mouth in judgment.

"Blessed is the one who reads aloud the words of this prophecy," Jake read, his voice stronger now. "How can this be a book of curses? It's surely a perfect tribute to God, not a way to invoke the Devil."

Morgan turned the pages carefully to chapter six, where the four Horsemen of the Apocalypse rode across the page.

"It's an exact match to the Thanatos tattoo," Morgan pointed at the pale horse's head braying to the heavens as Death rode it towards destruction.

"And they'll be searching for the original. We need to move," Jake replied.

"Just one more minute." Morgan turned the pages further to the end of Revelation where Marietti had said the curses were written, words that turned men into beasts capable of ripping another man to bloody chunks.

"Look, there are some pages are missing. The curses are gone and the images of the Devil and the Kingdom of Heaven aren't here."

There were torn stubs left behind, evidence that someone had tampered with the book. Jake bent to look more closely.

"You're right, they've been removed, and in a hurry by the look of the tears."

"So where are they?" asked Morgan. "We need to find them before Thanatos."

"For now, we need to get the book out of here," Jake said. "The next puzzle can wait."

Morgan nodded, her hand still lingering over the copper clasps that cornered the book.

"I saw a cleaning trolley in the hallway. I'll get that and we can wheel it out."

She retrieved the trolley and they hefted the book into it with the sackcloth as a protective hammock. They began to wheel it slowly back towards the main entrance, Jake still staggering every now and then with the pain in his head. Morgan felt the empty gaze of the corpses as an accusation, for they had disturbed the peace of the dead and blown apart their cadaverous children. She shuddered. Whether the book was cursed or not, this place felt as if the dead still lurked, wishing ill on those clinging to life. They reached the elevator and wheeled the trolley in as the door began to shut.

A gun thrust through the crack of the closing door, knocking it open again.

The Abbot stood there, his shrunken head a mask of despair but his eyes burning with fanaticism. He had seemed so harmless, so welcoming, but now Morgan could see that he had a hidden agenda, but she couldn't try to attack him, not with Jake so weak.

"You should have left," he said. "The explosion was a

warning, but now God has led me to the book through the destructive fire. I've been searching for the Devil's Bible and finally here it is." He indicated with the gun. "Get out and leave the trolley there."

"Who are you working for?" Jake whispered, his face grey and sweating now. Morgan could see he was suffering, and she helped him back out into the narrow corridor. The Abbot entered the elevator with the book, holding the gun towards them at all times.

"The one who will fulfill the prophecy and usher in the end times," he said as the door closed, leaving Morgan and Jake standing in the crypt with the carnage of the dead. Jake slumped down the wall as dizziness overcame him and put his head in his hands. Morgan banged her fists on the elevator door and tried to pry the doors open with desperate fingers. She rifled through her backpack, finding her phone but there was no reception this far underground. Marietti was expecting a call by 2am and if he didn't receive it, she knew he would send help after them.

She threw the pack down in frustration, angry that her first official mission with ARKANE had gone so badly wrong. Her partner was injured and the Devil's Bible taken by the agent of Thanatos. All they could do was sit here and wait for someone to get them out of the crypt. She sank down next to Jake as the flickering lights went out and they were left in darkness.

CHAPTER 16

Kutna Hora, Sedlec, Czech Republic. 2.03am

THE NIGHT CHILL HUNG like mist in the air as Natasha El-Behery stepped through the monastery gate, pulling the elegant cashmere shawl closer about her as she wheeled the heavy suitcase towards the church. She shivered, but tonight she was dressed to make an impression and a little cold wouldn't put her off.

The old Capuchin monk had delivered the Devil's Bible and had been eager for his reward, his only wish to finally meet his dark Lord. But Natasha was unwilling to share the glory of finding it with anyone, so she had taken him up in the helicopter with her and then pushed him out into the darkness of the Tyrrhenian Sea. She smiled as she remembered the utter surprise on his face as he fell into the darkness. Her smile spread as she thought of the reward she alone would surely receive tonight. Her shawl was a modest outer layer that could be shed quickly, given the opportunity. She was certain Milan would appreciate his gift enough that she would get to show him what was underneath. Her dress was tight, scarlet satin, smooth to the touch, hugging her curves while spike heels lengthened her legs. Tonight she had left her hair down, copper locks soft around her face for her encounters with Milan always left her wanting more.

There had been some rumors of what he had done to other women, but she could cope with a man like him, since her own passions also ran a little crooked.

Her heels clicked on the stone path as she walked towards the church, resolute in her mission. A light could be seen through the window but the door to the Gothic church was closed. Natasha knew Sedlec had originally been a monastery. In the thirteenth century, the abbot had journeyed to the Holy Land, returning with earth from Golgotha that he had scattered on the land surrounding the church. The cemetery thus became a desirable place to be buried. Forty thousand bodies had been poured into these pits over time, and now they decorated the church in macabre worship.

Natasha knocked at the door and heard measured footsteps inside. The door squeaked as it opened, and Natasha felt her heart rate rise. Milan Noble's face was lit by the electric lamp he held up and she was struck again by his classically handsome style.

"You have the book?" he asked, his smile cold in the dark. The pounding in Natasha's chest accelerated but her voice was calm as she replied.

"Of course." She smiled. "Are you going to let me in?"

He waved her past him, taking the suitcase handle from her, his need for it apparent. She squeezed past him in the doorframe and felt his warmth, his breath in her hair. She could feel he was taut with anticipation, barely controlling his desire to see the book. Once inside the church, the lamplight threw shadows amongst the bony sculptures, a palpable sense of loss permeating the place. Natasha turned back to see Milan bent over the suitcase, his hands greedily unwrapping the book. The Devil's Bible lay snugly protected and she could hear his breathing change as he realized it truly was the one he sought. He refastened the case, stood and came to stand next to her in the nave.

"Thank you for bringing it to me. This book drove my

father's desire and now drives mine."

"Your father?"

"Arkady Novotsky. He's buried in this graveyard. He was a great patron of this place and our family still has keys to the church and the crypt. Come, the Devil's Bible should be returned to where it belongs."

He turned and walked towards the altar where a flagstone had been lifted. He indicated that she should descend in front of him.

"Careful down these stairs, there's no railing."

Natasha stepped cautiously down into the darkness, her eyes adjusting to the faint light. Milan came down behind her, pulling the flagstone down into place with a thump and then rolling the suitcase carefully down behind him. He switched off the lamp.

"Stop there," he said. "Just breathe deeply for a minute. I want you to feel the essence of this place."

Natasha could hear him behind her as she did as he asked. He was close but not quite touching her. She inhaled slowly, smelling earth and stone, a damp musk. Images of the bones surrounding her pressed into her mind and the low ceiling seemed to crush the air down here. Then she felt his hand on her back, a light touch as if he was running one finger down her spine until he reached the curve of her buttocks. She wanted to press back against him but he stopped and the light flicked on.

"This is a sacred place, a secret I share only with you. Now let us see where the prophecy is written."

He stepped forward into the tiny room where Natasha could see a raised stone dais at one end. On it was a v-shaped stand of ancient wood, chestnut whorls enlivening it. Milan laid the case down reverently and Natasha heard him exhale, centering himself for this ritual moment. He only had eyes for the book as he opened the fabric that covered it. Natasha could see it had thick pages and heavy paper, encased in tooled leather with ornate metal clasps. The dirt of years had seeped intoit so the yellowing stain was made ivory in the lamplight. Milan looked at her, his eyes glazed and distant.

"This is it," he said. "The Codas Gigas, the biggest medieval manuscript in the world, the Devil's Bible and my inheritance. You've done well, Natasha. You will be rewarded, but now it must rest where it belongs. Help me."

Together they lifted the book from the suitcase and laid it onto the altar stand. Milan gently opened the first pages, his eyes wide, drinking in the fine detail of the book. As Natasha reached out to touch it, Milan took her hand and with it traced one of the images on the page, a saint tortured by demons with blood running down into a golden chalice.

"Curses and spells are drawn in the book as well as exorcism prayers. It's a Christian Bible but one that has been cursed and polluted over the centuries. It is the only sacred book with both holy words and demonic incantations." Natasha was hypnotized by Milan's voice. "The book belonged to Sedlec for many years, before it was moved to Prague and eventually stolen by the Swedes. The Vatican sowed false stories of where it had been hidden so you have shown great tenacity in finding it."

"It was indeed a pleasure." Natasha thought of the monk she had tortured and the abbot falling from sky to sea. She shivered in delight at the memories. "But why was your father so passionate about finding the Bible?"

Milan's voice was wistful.

"He believed that God had forsaken him and so he turned to the Devil, but in many ways he still clung to his faith. The prophecy was both a promise and a threat from God. He wanted to see the fulfillment of biblical truth but also the destruction of a world he saw as set against God." Milan began to turn the pages. "The prophecy and the curses are inscribed in the back where the Revelation of St John, the apocalypse, is written. The words give the reader power to usher in the final days. That's why I have continued my father's quest for the book."

He reached Revelation, then froze for a moment in horror and disbelief.

"What is this?" he shouted, turning on Natasha and grabbing her by the throat. "There are pages missing, torn from the book. Where are they? What have you done with them?"

Natasha could not speak with the crushing grip but her puzzled eyes must have given him pause as he released her. She fell to the floor, clutching her throat.

"I didn't know there were pages missing, I promise," she wheezed.

"Those pages are the key, the most important part of the book." He stood over her, his rage burning. "I can't do without them."

She could feel his latent violence about to explode but she wasn't afraid. Instead she would claim it. Natasha rose to her feet looking up at him, her body close to his as he stared down at her, chiseled jaw highlighted by the shadowed lamp, a face symmetrically perfect. His eyes were dark, a raging ocean with hidden depths, arms taut by his side.

"I brought you the book and I will bring you the stolen pages," she whispered. "Give me another chance."

Milan licked his lips, indecision flickering in his eyes but then he relaxed.

"I have waited long enough, so I can wait a little longer. You are a woman with similar appetites to my own so I believe I can trust your instincts to find the pages. You have your second chance."

He stroked a finger slowly across her chin and down the side of her neck, outlining the hieroglyphic tattoo that wound towards her back. He slid his finger down into the woolen wrap and pulled it away from her, then continued his journey, circling down over her breast, rubbing across her nipple, already hardened from the cold. He pinched it hard, twisting it a little, sublimating his violence into passion as she moaned her pleasure against his mouth.

DAY 4

CHAPTER 17

Blackfriars. Oxford, England. 11.12am

THE 'THOCK' OF CROQUET balls echoed around the summer green quadrangle as Morgan walked into the heart of Blackfriars College, the only functioning monastery in the city of Oxford. With the Devil's Bible stolen, Morgan needed to know what Father Ben Costanza was keeping from her, in case it could shed some light on where they should start looking for the mysterious Thanatos organization. After the humiliation of having to be rescued from Palermo by Marietti's backup team, she needed to make up time and hasten the search for the missing pages. Her old friend and mentor had helped her and ARKANE with the Pentecost stones, but he also kept a secret which he had only hinted at so far. She needed to know what he was hiding.

As she reached the stone stairwell to the tiny office, Morgan took a deep breath. The last time she had been here, men from Thanatos had stormed the college, killing students and monks as well as burning the offices. Some redecoration had been completed but there was still evidence here and there in the bullet-chipped stone and blackened pillars. Morgan headed up the stairs. Ben's office door was open and she paused at the entrance to watch the old man writing, back bent over his work as the faint sounds of college life filtered through the windows.

"Still writing by hand I see," Morgan said as she walked in. Ben turned and his face broke into a smile, then clouded a little with guilt and concern. He pushed his chair back and opened his arms.

"Come here, child. I've missed you. Where have you been hiding?"

Morgan smiled and walked into his arms. His embrace was as close to a father's now her own was gone. Ben had been her parents' friend and continued as her mentor and ally within the walls of Oxford University which could close ranks on newcomers. Her colleagues had often made her feel like a fraud, before Ben had eased her fears with his in-depth knowledge of University politics.

"You've redecorated," she said, releasing the embrace and looking around at his bookcase which had been gunned to pieces the last time she had left this office.

"Yes, and with some grant money I managed to obtain for special services, the college has agreed to forget about the whole affair. I have ARKANE to thank for cleaning up the mess. But enough of that. Are you alright, Morgan? How are Faye and lovely little Gemma?"

Morgan sank down into one of the old leather armchairs as Ben shuffled over and put the kettle on. He had a little tea-making kit in here and liked his own blend of chai, steeped with cinnamon, cardamom and a kick of ginger spice.

"I'm trying to keep them away from any more adventures," replied Morgan. "But I'm part of a team on the trail of Thanatos now and I need to know about the past, Ben."

Ben's back stiffened and he remained silent as he stirred the sweet chai. When he spoke, his words were heavy with regret.

"It's an old tale, but perhaps time you knew it. Maybe it will help you with the present. When I recognized the image of the pale horse, I knew I had to tell you but finding the right moment has been hard." Passing her tea, he eased himself down opposite her. "This is how it was when I knew your parents nearly thirty-five years ago."

Ephesus, Turkey. August 1977

"Ben, come and look at this. I think I might have found something."

The voice carried across the still heat of the day and I lifted my head at the musical Welsh accent. Marianne could always get my attention and it was a welcome break from the meticulous brushing of ancient buried stone. I climbed out of the trench I had been clearing and walked over to look down into the pit where she was working. We were digging near the Library of Celsus, built in the first century and thought to have once contained thousands of scrolls. At that time, Ephesus was one of the greatest cities in the Roman Empire, so these ruined buildings were just part of the ancient cityscape. There had been a tiny but growing Christian group here living in fear of Roman persecution and we were searching for a cache of artifacts from that time. A reference had been found to the cache in the Vatican archives and a small team of archaeologists had been sent to investigate which I had joined on a mini sabbatical from my studies at Blackfriars College. As I specialized in early Church history, I was thrilled to have the opportunity to search for such potentially significant artifacts. However, I felt that my role was uncertain as I had joined the team so late in the season. The relationships between the others had formed prior to my arrival and only Marianne had tried to make me feel welcome.

"What have you found?" I asked. She looked up at me, her green eyes alight with excitement. I saw past the dirty streaks on her clothes and earth smudged across her cheeks. Her golden hair was tied back into a long plait, hidden under the hat that shielded her eyes. Her fair skin was protected by the long sleeves and baggy trousers she wore, but nothing could hide those emerald eyes and dirt couldn't obscure her radiance.

"I think it's a tablet explaining part of the journey of the apostles. Come down and have a look."

I jumped down into the pit, then bent to examine the tablet. It had only been partially uncovered but I could read some of the ancient Greek letters. I was aware of how close Marianne was. She smelled of the fertile earth, wet clay and also of the heat, the sweat of the dig. I leaned closer and my arm brushed hers.

"What do you think?" she asked. "Your ancient Greek is better than mine."

"I don't think so," I replied with a smile. I knew she was just humoring me as she had a DPhil in Classics from Oxford University and her Greek was flawless. I traced the letters with a finger. "It reads like the beginning of a letter to the early Church. What's this word?"

"It's lamp-stand," Marianne grinned in triumph.

"Seriously, then this could be ... "

"Yes, one of the letters to the church in Ephesus as mentioned in Revelation 2. It talks about removing the lamp-stand if they don't return to the faithful practices of the church. This could be the start of the cache, Ben. This is so exciting. These are the moments we live for as archaeologists."

She grabbed my hands and did a kind of happy dance in the confines of the trench, laughing as she twirled under my arm. I was briefly in heaven and locked that moment in my mind. God forgive me for the thoughts I had about her, set against all the vows I had taken.

"Get over to the main findings tent, you two. There's no time for that now."

The voice came from above and we both looked up to see Arkady Novotsky staring down at us, a frown on his aristocratic face.

Marianne protested.

"But Arkady, look what we've … "

"There's no time for this. We're not here for documents, for worthless tablets. I've had a communication and need to share it with the team. Main tent, ten minutes."

He stomped off and his shadow retreated in the heat of the afternoon sun.

Marianne rolled her eyes at me.

"He seems to be getting worse, don't you think?"

I nodded.

"If we're not here for tablets like this, then what are we here for?"

Marianne's smile faded and her eyes darkened. She turned in the narrow trench and I caught sight of her profile. Her rounded belly protruded significantly now, reminding me that she could never be mine. She rubbed at it absent-mindedly.

"Sometimes I'm not even sure myself, but I suppose we should get to the main tent. I'm going to need your help getting out of this trench."

She cheerily tried to distract me but I was puzzled. This tablet could possibly be significant but Arkady had dismissed it as nothing. What was going on here? I smiled at Marianne, hiding the mixed emotions I held in check every time I looked at her.

"Let's get you out of here then," I said, helping her up the ladder.

The main camp tent was dark inside, a welcome respite from the harsh Turkish sun. The canvas cast a green light over the people inside, as if they were under a rainforest canopy. Conversation was muted as the team gathered to wait for the announcement. I followed Marianne as she went to sit with her husband, Leon Sierra, a ruggedly handsome Sephardic Jew. I knew Leon had been born in Spain and was now living in Israel between archaeological digs. He was confident and loved a good argument, which I had experienced around the campfire most evenings. When Leon turned his attention on you, he made you feel unique. When he turned away, it was as if the face of God had moved on, his favors bestowed on someone else. The spell he had cast on Marianne was complete because his attention was still fixed on her, but I worried for her future. What would happen when his attentions were focused elsewhere? They surely would, as the brilliant man had a short attention span, flitting between projects, solving archaeological mysteries and then moving on. Leon was a true citizen of the nascent state of Israel, bent on finding his place in the world and willing to fight in order to protect it.

Marianne sat down heavily and Leon pulled her into him, reaching out to stroke her stomach.

"Neshama Sheli," he spoke softly but I could still hear the words. The Hebrew meant 'my soul' and the endearment hurt me, even though I knew I had no right to feel this way. I tried to focus on the other people gathering in the tent, willing myself away from their intimacy, but I couldn't stop myself thinking about them. I knew that Leon and Marianne had met on last summer's dig right here in Ephesus. Their passion had exploded and they married fast. Now she was five months pregnant with twins. Marianne had said they were returning to Israel after the dig was finished. She had looked wistful as she spoke, but it seemed that Leon couldn't stand the winter in her native Wales and so they wouldn't go back this year.

Arkady strode into the tent, flinging the canvas violently open before him. He launched into a tirade immediately, not bothering to wait until everyone was seated.

"We've spent three months here and what do we have to show for it?" He pointed at one of the display tables, where some tablets and pottery shards lay. "We're not here for coins or pots or useless tablets. We're here for the relics of the early Church. We're here for clues as to where the most precious objects might be."

I had never seen Arkady like this before. The man had previously been fair and even tempered but now spittle flew from his mouth as he spat his words.

"Where Hitler failed in finding the greatest relics, we will succeed. Ephesus may be where the Apostle John wrote his gospel. This is the site of one of the seven churches of Revelation. This is where three separate early ecclesiastical councils met to decide on the beliefs of the Church. Yet we have pitifully little to show for our time here. We've found practically nothing and time is running out."

A man dressed completely in black stepped forward and calmly placed his hand on Arkady's arm. The gesture seemed at once a dominant warning, but also fatherly, although the man seemed barely a few years older than Arkady.

Marianne whispered to me.

"That's Elias Marietti, the liaison from the Vatican secret archives. All very hush-hush."

Arkady calmed and changed his tone. The man removed his hand.

"We have funding for only two more weeks and then we're done for the season," he said. "I'm sorry but the funding for Ephesus is being channeled into a new project for next year. Some of you may be asked to join but it will be quite a different journey."

An audible groan went up from the gathered team, many of whom needed the meager pay the dig provided. The end of this project meant the end of a fixed income for most and they would have to return to other jobs for the off-season. Arkady opened the floor for questions and hands went up all over the tent.

"I'm going to go back and examine that tablet," I whispered to Marianne. "If it's important, perhaps it can help keep the dig open for longer."

She nodded, but her face was clouded, her eyes misty and focused on Arkady. Her hand was tightly grasping Leon's. I left the tent without looking back for it was not my career that was at stake, and I suddenly felt like an outsider once again.

Later that evening, I waited until the camp was quiet and then picked my way back towards Arkady's tent. I had fully excavated and cleaned up the tablet and I was convinced it was related to the Revelation letter to the Ephesus church. The language was similar to the Greek used in the New Testament prophecy and also in the gospel of John. If it could be matched, then surely this was the beginning of something more significant? I had to return to Blackfriars within a few months and I was desperate to go back with an experience of something bigger than the closeted life of an academic monk. If I was honest with myself, I also wanted to stay near Marianne a little longer. She brought a glimmer of magic to my life.

I'd been agonizing for hours over how to approach Arkady, given the mood he seemed to be in, but I knew this was my last chance. Most of the team would give up quickly and look for other work. Ephesus had a number of dig sites and they would all be jostling for position with other teams. I walked past Leon and Marianne's tent and heard voices raised in anger. Leon spoke in fast Spanish, in turns annoyed, frustrated and then pleading. Emotion could be understood across any language gap. I stood still for a moment, wondering whether I should intervene. I could hear Marianne crying and then Leon's voice soften as he clearly went to comfort her. The sounds soon became more intimate and I walked away, my shoulders dropping. I prayed for the strength to be faithful to my vows made to the Dominican order. Help me obey, Lord. Forgive these treacherous thoughts, I prayed. I knew that the vows didn't exclude me from these feelings but I knew that a higher purpose was meant for me. I was a teacher and a student of Sacred Theology and this summer interlude was a brief sojourn, intended to teach me new lessons. I was certainly learning them.

I arrived at Arkady's tent. The flap was partially open and I could see inside where Arkady sat at his desk, back to the doorway. He was surrounded by sketches, pieces of paper covered in drawings and some thrown to the floor. Many were crumpled and torn, others discarded, only half drawn but all of them featured a horse's head in black charcoal, its nostrils flared and eyes wild. In some, the torso of the horse was shown and in one, a rider could be seen, a skeletal figure reaching down with a sword towards a victim huddled at its feet. A bottle of Raki sat near Arkady's right arm, the cheap Turkish aniseed alcohol that I had seen the locals drinking on a Saturday night. The bottle was almost empty and as I watched, Arkady filled his glass again, downed the spirit and continued to draw. His arm moved fast and he was a surprisingly good artist, dashing out the sketches and then drawing again on another piece of thick white paper. I could see obsession in the man's movements, the edge of darkness in his drawings. This was not the time to talk to Arkady

Novotsky, so I walked away into the humid Turkish night.

"That was the first time I saw the figure of the pale horse, the stylized head that Thanatos now uses as its symbol. I didn't see it again until the attack by the team before Pentecost." Ben pointed at the wall where the graffiti of the braying horse had been spray-painted during the assault only a few weeks ago. "It was left on my wall and that's when I knew I would have to tell you the truth about that time."

"Did you ever get to speak to Arkady about the tablet?"

"No," replied Ben. "The next day he left with Marietti and everything wound up soon after."

"So what happened to Arkady later?" Morgan asked.

"He was one of those on the 1979 trip to recover the Nazi treasures supposedly hidden in Antarctica. Marietti led that expedition and soon after he left the Vatican to head up the ARKANE Institute."

Morgan frowned, puzzled.

"Surely that trip was a myth? Could Hitler really have smuggled the occult treasures out before the end of the war?"

"That expedition happened alright, but it was done in top secret. I only know because of your mother. It seemed that Leon had been asked to go but in the end he was one too many fiery personalities. He stormed off before the expedition left and never worked with that team again. You and Faye had been born by then and Marianne had made a lovely little home for you in Oxford where she had a lecturing job. But Leon never settled and they separated."

Morgan sighed.

"I can't believe you didn't tell me this before. You had nothing to be scared of, Ben and you weren't part of their breakup. I worshipped my father, but I know he had his faults and a hell of a temper."

Ben bent his head and looked at the floor. He struggled to find the right words to tell her the final piece of the puzzle.

"I loved your mother, Morgan. She was the love of my life. Of course that love was never consummated and I never told her. But she knew. I couldn't help but be happy when Leon left, as then Marianne needed my help. We were friends, close friends. I'm so sorry." Ben's hand clutched Morgan's arm, like an anchor in his storm of emotion. "I've felt this guilt for a long time as I celebrated the breakup of your family, and God forgive me for it, but I loved the years I had as her close confidante. Faye never warmed to me, but when you came to Oxford, I felt as if Marianne was smiling on our friendship."

Morgan stood up and paced the small office, then returned and knelt in front of him. She took his old hands in hers.

"Ben, you were a good friend to the mother I never knew. What happened back then is in the past. You're my friend now and you also know vital clues to what might be going on, so I need you to be honest with me. Life moves on, we all change."

"I don't believe Marietti has changed," Ben replied. "Which is why I worry for you working with ARKANE." He waved his hand, as if to brush away the past. "But no matter, you must make your own decision."

"Did Arkady continue to work for Marietti?" Morgan asked.

"No, they had a violent difference of opinion on the Antarctica trip. Arkady never worked well with others anyway, especially if he wasn't in charge. He became dangerously obsessed with the occult. Marianne told me that he coveted the treasures they sought and spent a great deal of time studying the black arts."

Ben walked to the window, looking out at the summer

rain that had cleared the quad. "Then something serious happened and Marietti severed all ties with him."

Morgan waited for him to continue.

"Arkady had become involved with a girl, Aniela, very young and beautiful. Few had seen her, as she mainly stayed hidden in his rooms, and no one was friends with her. Poor girl, so isolated. She was found one morning, strangled, badly beaten and cut in what looked like a ritual pattern. It seemed the occult had turned Arkady's mind."

"Was he arrested?" Morgan asked.

Ben turned, shaking his head.

"It was covered up, considered too high a risk for the expedition to have a police investigation. After all, they sought occult objects and it was a religious trip funded partially by the Vatican secret archives. Aniela was Polish with no family they could trace. So her body was cremated and Arkady was just sent away."

"But he was clearly a dangerous man? What happened to him after that?"

"I only found out about it later but I ask forgiveness for what happened daily. Marianne always worried that he would come after you or Faye, and when she died, she made me promise to always watch over you. When I saw the braying horse's head, the sign of Thanatos, it made me think that Arkady had returned. I hadn't seen that sign for many years and now here it is again, in a new incarnation."

"But what connects Thanatos to Arkady? He would be an old man or maybe dead now?"

Ben sighed.

"Later on he had a family and a son but he remained obsessed with the prophecy. I believe that this is the beginning of the fulfillment of Arkady's dark plan started long ago and the son has found a way to take the plot global."

"How can you be sure?" Morgan asked. "No one has that kind of global reach."

Ben picked up a glossy magazine and handed it to her. The front page was emblazoned with the angular face of Milan Noble, CEO of Zoebios. The glowing lead article extolled the virtues of the multi-billion dollar pharmaceutical business that had expanded from the West into Africa, and now China and India. It portrayed Noble as the 'Lord of Life', a man on the brink of changing the world with his focus on birth control, education for women, mental as well as physical health.

"He's the spitting image of Arkady," Ben said. "I look at him and it's as if I'd just walked off the dig. If Arkady's son runs that company, then he has the power to change the world. He holds the health of millions in his hands, Morgan. You need to find out if he's behind Thanatos and what he's up to before he unleashes the prophecy on those he's meant to serve."

CHAPTER 18

London, England. 1.13pm

MICHAEL JENSEN ROLLED OVER in bed and looked at the time again. The cheap blue digital watch had a cracked plastic cover but at least it still worked. It had only been two hours since the last pill but they helped to quell his anger and he wanted to experience the sensation once more. Without the pills the audio program had made him feel calm and relaxed, affording him a brief space of sanity in an increasingly crazy world. That was addictive enough, but the new pills and the headset made him feel as if he was in the presence of the Divine and he wanted that feeling again. The note that had come with the couriered package said that the pills should be taken once daily before the audio for the full effect. But what harm could come from being in that place for a longer period? It was as if the clouds had parted in his mind and he could perceive more than the human eye could see. He was like an eagle soaring above the earth, and the voice that spoke made him feel chosen.

Michael hadn't thought much about God since he was a teenager. A brief flirtation with a Christian youth club provided him with girlfriends but certainly no inner belief. He had answered the questions on the Zoebios website saying that he was a Christian but it had been years since he had been to church. Still, the stories from Sunday school stuck with him and he had prayed at times of desperation. He knew that he was responsible for where he was now, but that didn't make it any easier. He'd lost his job at the factory when his anger had spilled over one time too many after repeated warnings and in this economy, it was proving hard to find other work.

At the beginning, he had been to the Job Centre every day, determined to beat the odds, sure that he wouldn't be just another statistic. But then it had become harder and harder to get up, as he had nothing to show for his efforts, so what was the point of trying anymore? As Michael reached for the pills, he looked at the picture by the bed. Jenny's smile had been real back then, before he had driven her away. He glanced over at the door, splintered in places where he had punched and kicked it in frustration. He clenched his fists as the anger rose again.

But in the last few days he had felt some hope. The audios he had downloaded from Zoebios had made him start to think that he could change something, that his actions could make a difference. The pills supercharged the feeling so how could it be a bad thing if he took more now? He popped a pill from the packet, placed it under his tongue and put on the large headset. Michael started to feel a presence as he listened, an entity that was just out of the corner of his eye. He sensed it was there but now he wanted to see it. Was it God? Was he seeing the manifestation of Jesus?

Here in North London, faith was a complicated thing. He was only a few streets from the Finsbury Park mosque where extremist Islamic clerics had once preached a message of hate. Michael had always considered the Muslims he worked with as his friends, but then he had seen them keep their jobs when he lost his. Perhaps Britain should be only for the truly British after all.

As the audio played, it seemed that God was speaking to

him directly, and the things He said resonated with Michael's own feelings of increasing isolation. He talked about how the Muslims weren't like us, they deserved to die. Look at the terror they had inflicted on the world and how they were marginalizing British people in their own country. The music behind the words changed tempo and became a call to arms, a thumping in Michael's blood. Where there had been peace and calm, he now found empowerment for his deep seated anger, a rage that could explode into violence and a target that was now identified. As the drugs raced through his system he listened to the words of God, his fists tightening in anticipation.

New York, USA. 9.12am

Shahzia Mohammad sat in the tiny bathroom and put the new headset on. It was the only place she felt private, as if Kamil could feel she had been doing something forbidden in any other room even when he wasn't there. She ignored the stained bathtub and cracked sink and pretended the hard toilet seat was a soft cushion. She pushed one of the tiny pills from the packet and swallowed it, her throat catching in her haste to get it down. She needed the calm the audios brought her and she trusted that the new pills would just enhance the experience.

Shahzia had identified as Muslim on the Zoebios site so she knew the program would be appropriate for her. It had to be better than the women at the health center who preached Jesus in one breath and insulted her in the next. She pressed Play on the tiny mp3 player, closed her eyes and let peace wash around her like a warm pool. It strengthened her and made her feel safe. She had tried to blend into this

American world, so far from her own, but she desperately missed her mother and sisters. She knew Kamil wanted his children to be brought up as true Americans with no trappings of the past, but her own anxiety had grown because she had no anchor for her life. There was no longer any ritual or extended family to ground their new life in this alien place. Their roots were growing in thin soil here and she didn't know how to make things better.

As Shahzia relaxed she began to feel a presence with her in the tiny bathroom, a glimmer of someone or something hovering just out of reach. The God of her childhood had been there when she was afraid; maybe now He had come back to help her again. She began to pray fervently, rocking back and forth on the seat. It squeaked rhythmically but Shahzia didn't notice. Her words were desperate pleas for God to help her, to show her the path. How could she change this life in which she had found herself?

Suddenly she stopped rocking. She could hear words now, faint but surely coming from God himself. He spoke of how she could change her life, show her obedience and make a difference. An image filled Shahzia's mind of St Mary's Catholic School, the bowed heads of rich white Christians in the classroom overlooking the road. She walked past it every day, taking her own two girls to the predominantly Muslim school a few blocks away. Shahzia felt bile rise in her throat. She felt sick at what she was being asked to do but it seemed that God himself wanted her to act. He wanted her to be an instrument of his judgment and this school was the way she could show her obedience.

CHAPTER 19

British Museum, London, England. 6.41pm

AS THE EVENING SUN cast lengthy shadows across
the courtyard, Morgan walked up the steps to the British
Museum. Tonight's event was a private viewing for a collection of religious relics where the gruesome manner of
the saints' death was depicted in excruciating detail on the
caskets that held the grisly mementoes. Morgan had been
an advisor for the research on the psychological motivation of martyrs, and although it had been months since she
had been part of the University team, she now needed the
connection for the investigation. With Ben's tentative recognition of Arkady's son, she needed evidence that Milan
Noble was the one they sought. Marietti wouldn't normally
have sanctioned any overt investigation into the multinational CEO without further evidence, but his own past with
Arkady Novotsky had forced the Director's hand.

The Museum also had experts in medieval manuscripts,
some of which were in the collection tonight, so Morgan
hoped to gain some insight into where the missing pages of
the Devil's Bible might be. She had seen from the advance
publicity that the Zoebios Foundation was one of the major
donors and Milan Noble had been particularly interested in
this exhibition. He had even called in favors to help source

some of the reliquaries from churches that would have otherwise refused to lend their treasures. Milan would be there tonight and Morgan intended to see what he was like in person. Given the setting, there was no danger so she went independently, much to Jake's chagrin at being left behind.

Checking her coat, she walked into the great hall of the museum, lit from above by the vast skylights. Even though it was nearly seven, the sun still lit the cream colored walls of the rotunda. Passing into one of the museum's great halls, Morgan took a glass of Semillon Blanc from one of the waiting staff and walked through the giant basalt pillars into the Enlightenment Gallery. There were a few early patrons wandering the high ceilinged hall, speaking in hushed whispers and clutching their glasses of wine. This was one of Morgan's favorite places in the Museum, representing the age of reason, discovery and learning, a time when men had wanted to unlock the mysteries of the universe by studying natural and man-made objects. Great collectors, some would say pillagers, wanted to classify and catalogue, to understand and control their environment.

This room contained objects from all over the known world and Morgan began a slow circle of discovery, since there was time before the speeches began and the new exhibition was opened. She ran her fingers over the surface of the Rosetta Stone, gently skimming the words in hieroglyphics, Greek and cuneiform. This stone had unlocked the knowledge of ancient Egypt, enabling the revelation of treasure and curses buried for generations. Civilizations with no writing die, Morgan thought, with no way of finding out what they believed, or how they lived. In a way, it was as if they hadn't even existed. It was part of the reason to come to the museum, a kind of memento mori, a reminder of the short span of our existence, to make the most of our time before we become dust. She passed by a Sati stone, an 18th century sandstone memorial to an Indian wife who had thrown herself onto the pyre of her husband. Morgan shuddered at the knowledge that most went unwillingly and the brief reminder of how Pentecost could have ended for her twin sister, Faye, immolated on top of a madman's pyre.

The walls were lined with books in glass fronted cases that rose to the balcony and then up to the ceiling. Morgan gazed into the cabinets, wishing she could take the books from the shelves and delve into their crumbling pages. 'The History of British India' and 'Lives of the Queens of England' lined up next to bricks from ancient Babylon inscribed with the name of Nebuchadnezzar. This was a treasure house of collective memory that resonated across time.

Morgan bent over another case where precious stones had been burnt and shriveled from a great heat. This was considered evidence of the divine retribution that befell the Biblical Near East, evidence of God's punishment when fire rained down on the sinful cities. Morgan smiled. We see whatever we want in these ancient stones, she thought, but that is the beauty of the past, for we can read into it our own fate. In another cabinet were wax seals from the astrologer and mathematician John Dee, known as the magician of Queen Elizabeth I. They were inscribed with occult symbols for conjuring divine spirits. The thousands of years separating these objects demonstrated that humans never changed. They will always grasp after the supernatural, a glimpse of the divine, and a reason for this brutish and short existence.

Morgan caught sight of the Curator, standing talking to a man who must be Milan Noble at the front of the room. They were near the podium, preparing to speak. The Curator looked up and caught her eye, lifting a hand in a brief wave as Milan followed his gaze and Morgan felt him look at her. She didn't meet his eyes but waved briefly back to the Curator in recognition as a small bell rang and the Museum chairwoman rose to speak.

"Good evening. It is with great pleasure that I welcome

you here tonight, as respected and important supporters of the Museum. This collection could not have been brought together without your support. Tonight we acknowledge in particular the generosity of the Zoebios Foundation."

At this she turned and acknowledged Milan Noble, who bowed slightly from the waist, giving a charming smile.

"And now ladies and gentleman, here is the Curator, who will tell you about the collection."

Morgan sipped her wine as the Curator spoke about the relics. She watched Milan Noble, his attention focused on the speaker. He was built like a sprinter with sleek powerful muscles under a charcoal tailored suit and his racing green tie matched his striking eyes. His jaw was just as chiseled as the magazines portrayed. A gorgeous man and an enigma, apparently single and reclusive, but what could possibly interest the CEO of a multinational health organization in an exhibition on ancient Christian relics?

"And now, please feel free to enter the exhibition and do let us know if you have any questions."

The Curator finished speaking to the restrained applause of those around and small groups started to move towards the exhibits. Morgan could see Milan busy in conversation, so she drifted in with a party of academics. The collection was housed within a great dome constructed in the middle of the entry hall of the Museum. The vaulted ceiling with hues of aquamarine and deep indigo was lit with tiny spotlights, and dotted with scarlet crosses. Looking up, Morgan felt it was like looking into a sky flecked with blood.

The exhibition was organized into a timeline of faith, from the early Christians who were persecuted and killed, to the time of Thomas à Becket and beyond. The deaths of the Christian martyrs were gruesome and imaginative: torn apart by wool combs, roasted on griddles, devoured by wild animals as well as death by crucifixion. The bones were collected by the faithful and divided up before being sent to rest at churches all over the world. People who worshipped there would have only been aware of the relic they had; they wouldn't have seen the millions of others. But in this collection alone, it was clear how much forgery was a part of the relic business. How many bones from the body of St James were there? How many pieces of the true cross were worshipped?

Morgan stopped in front of a huge reliquary. Over a meter long, it contained two hundred compartments, each with a small package of silk containing a relic labeled with the name of the saint from whom it came. Parchment labels in spindly writing were tied to the little parcels. It reminded her of a kind of spiritual pick'n'mix, a sweet shop of saints' remains. She leaned in to look more closely.

"Fascinating, isn't it?"

Morgan turned to see Milan Noble next to her, a glass of champagne in his hand. "How many of those pieces of bone do you think were from real martyrs?" he asked in a quiet voice.

"I was just wondering that myself," she smiled up at him. He was significantly taller than her, even in her heels.

"Milan Noble," he said, stretching out his hand.

She shook it firmly, looking him boldly in the eye, ever one to meet the challenge.

"Dr Morgan Sierra, and I do know who you are."

He raised an eyebrow, humor sparkling in his green eyes.

"I can hardly keep a low profile these days. I thought perhaps I could stay away from the crowd at this event since no one is here for the living. And why are you here, Dr Sierra?"

Morgan turned back to the cabinet.

"I consulted for the team who wrote the texts for the exhibits and I know Samuel, the Curator. He and I even worked on some exhibits in Israel and please, do call me

Morgan."

Milan smiled, and leaned towards her. She could smell his cologne, subtle, with notes of lapsang-souchong tea, smoky and intoxicating. Morgan felt a magetism in his attention, a dangerous eddy under his immaculate exterior.

"So what do you think of these relics?" he asked. "Is this just an art exhibition or is there something to this kind of belief?"

Morgan hesitated and the brief moment of thought was filled by the music that played in the chamber, a religious chant of monks extolling the virtues of God in the Alleluya, Dulce Ligname, Dulces Clavos.

"That's a difficult question," she replied. "There are still martyrs today and people believe the bones of saints continue to perform miracles. The bones of the holy have always been honored in some way, but I find it a strange mix of deep rooted belief and cynical profiteering. Like this." She indicated a gold reliquary. "You can see St Lawrence being roasted slowly on a grill saying as his flesh burns, 'turn me over so the other side can cook as well'. Then you have all his bones, sold so that the church could fill their coffers. It turns my stomach in a physical sense even while I'm fascinated by the psychology behind it."

Milan's gaze was penetrating and Morgan found that she wanted to look away from those eyes.

"Cynical perhaps on the part of the Church," he said. "But these people died for their true faith. Perhaps they could see a reward in heaven that was better than their days on earth?"

"I'm sure they did, but the glorification of their suffering was trumpeted by those educated enough to escape that type of death. Who knows what the true story was behind the deaths of these martyrs?"

They strolled around the exhibits together, walking in companionable silence. Morgan felt that Milan exuded a repressed energy, like a force field he was reining in.

"There is a story," he said as they stopped at one of the glass cases. "It is perhaps apocryphal, but it might interest you. In 1190, the Bishop of Lincoln visited the Abbey of Fecamp in Normandy to venerate the monastery's greatest treasure, an arm bone of Mary Magdalene. It wasn't enough for him to see it in its silk wrapping. He demanded to see the bone itself in order to kiss it. To the horror of the monks, he tried to break off a piece, then began to gnaw at the bone and eventually broke off splinters which he pocketed to take back to his own church."

"Oh, that's disgusting," Morgan said and they both laughed. "Exactly why I have severe doubts about these relics."

"Perhaps, but he was defiant in his faith and claimed that he had honored the saint as Christians venerated Christ when they ate his flesh and drank his blood at Communion."

Morgan found Milan intriguing. Clearly he had a deep interest in this realm of relics, a strange fascination and one she shared. But there was still no evidence that he was behind Thanatos and she needed to focus on her reason for being there.

Milan steered her towards a case containing a gold filigree cross studded with garnets.

"You would look beautiful wearing this, Dr Sierra."

Morgan gazed in at the cross and smiled.

"I love the garnet, but did you know that the colors of the stones have a spiritual meaning as well? The garnet and ruby are the blood of Christ, the amethyst invoked to staunch the flow of blood, the sapphire for the holy blue of the Virgin and heaven itself."

"The question is whether there is actually any residual power in the physical form of the relic," Milan said. "Part of my funding for these relics and their research is to test samples of the bones and blood to see if they are special in some way. Is there some primal power that we can use? For Zoebios research purposes of course. If we can find the miraculous at the cellular level, we could use it to improve the human race."

"Really, and have you found anything yet?" Morgan asked, trying to hide her shock at his words. Perhaps there was some hidden aspect of eugenics behind Zoebios.

"We have some interesting investigations in progress," Milan continued. "But we keep the research and results quiet because much of what we find would invalidate the claims of many of these relics. If for example, these aren't the bones of a first century saint, and those thorns date from 600AD, would that impact people's belief?"

"I don't think that matters much to true believers. It's more about faith," Morgan replied.

Milan grasped her elbow lightly and led her on. His touch on her skin was possessive in a way Morgan couldn't define, and yet she didn't shrink from it. They walked together through the final room of the exhibition which held the relics of Thomas à Becket, the famous English martyr slaughtered after his fight with King Henry II in 1170. Morgan examined one of the golden scenes that showed the saint praying as his head was cleaved open by the blow of a sword. The soldier then scooped the brains out onto the floor of Canterbury Cathedral. The monks had collected the blood and bodily fluids, diluted and stored it in flasks and sold it to the faithful. Thomas was canonized soon after his murder and Canterbury soon became one of the most popular and venerated pilgrimage routes, the basis of Chaucer's Canterbury tales. The shrine was destroyed in the iconoclasm, the destruction of religious images carried out under Henry VIII, but some of the saint's body was saved and displayed in the church.

They were almost at the end of the display and Morgan knew she needed some indication that Milan was involved in the recent events. She couldn't go back to ARKANE with nothing.

"Why are you so personally interested in relics?" she asked. "I thought your company was a promoter of life and health?"

"What is life if not the flip-side of death?" Milan replied. "Look at how obsessed the public is with dismemberment, death and decay. There are bodies and bones in forensic shows, violent crime novels and films. We are obsessed with it." Milan turned and gazed into the last cabinet as he spoke, "I have always been interested in the entwined dependence of life and death. They often meet in religion, where everlasting life is promised on bodily death but where physical life is squandered. Religion preaches the sanctity of life even as it destroys."

"Death isn't remarkable, and neither is life, in the grand scheme of things," Morgan replied. "It's only when you look at an individual life that meaning can be seen in these special moments. Your company seems to be helping those who are struggling, so you must believe life is precious?"

Milan seemed to be hypnotized by the gold that glinted from the reliquary of St Thomas, and he spoke in low, mesmerizing tones.

"Eros and Thanatos, the life and death instincts, they rage inside us all." He stopped abruptly. "Now Dr Sierra … Morgan … I must go. It has been marvelous to meet you and I hope very much to see you again."

He shook her hand, snake green eyes challenging hers, and then strode off towards the exit, a head taller than those around him. Morgan stood speechless in front of the display case. The use of the word Thanatos had taken her by surprise. Could the 'Lord of Life' really be involved with the death of others?

DAY 5

CHAPTER 20

London, England. 11.18am

THE SUN WAS ALREADY high and Michael Jensen was trying to keep cool in his bulky coat as he sat in the shade of a chestnut tree on a tiny grassy patch opposite Finsbury Park mosque. It fitted easily into the suburban landscape with its red brick exterior and minimal white minaret. There seemed to be some kind of festival and he could hear the sound of chanted prayers as large groups of people entered as he watched. The school holidays meant there were many children and young people in the crowd, some obviously dragged there by their parents but others hurried ahead, keen in their youthful devotion. Michael felt a jealousy as he watched the banter between friends and close knit families going in together for he had never felt part of such a community, even as a young man. A little boy ran along the street ahead of his parents who turned to each other in pride, their love for each other evident even as they kept several paces apart.

Michael suddenly felt that what he was about to do must be wrong. How could the killing of children be sanctioned? Yet he must obey the highest authority and who was he to question the commands of God? To calm himself, he pulled on the headset and pressed Play on the mp3 player, urging the sensations to fill him again. He thought he'd taken the entire pill packet this morning but the details were fuzzy, colors brighter and time super speedy. The courier who had delivered the pills had also handed him a bulky package.

"You'll know what to do with it," the man had said before leaving. Michael had been so desperate to get back into the presence of God that he had taken the pills immediately and plugged himself into the newly downloaded audio files. Pounding music had filled his brain and this time the God of War emerged, battle ready and with a mission that only Michael could fulfill. Outside the mosque he re-entered that state of readiness with the buzz of the drugs dulling the sensation in his body. At the same time they heightened his perception to light and sound, the immensity and beauty of the world about to be opened wide to the cosmos.

Michael opened his coat slightly and flicked the countdown button. It showed 70 seconds ... 69 ... 68 ... 67 ...

Michael turned up the audio to full volume ... 52 ... 51...

He ran across the road and into the open door of the mosque, passing the last families arriving behind him...39...38...37...

There were shouts as people tried to tackle him, screams as someone shouted a warning. Michael ran into the main prayer hall, shouldering his way through. It was packed with people. They turned with surprise ... 19 ... 18 ...

He could see their lips moving in prayer but the soundtrack in his head played only war and rage. The little boy who had been skipping outside knelt next to his father. For a moment, Michael wished his task away but the pounding in his head increased to a crescendo. I will obey, Lord, he thought, closing his eyes as the bomb tore his earthly body apart.

New York, USA. 9.15am

Shahzia Mohammad knew she had phoned the Zoebios helpline the previous night to ask for more pills, but the large package that had arrived that morning puzzled her. The twinge of anxiety was quashed when she found the pills and she tore into the packet, desperate to re-enter the state of grace she had felt in the presence of the Divine. For a short time it felt as if nothing was important except the infinitesimal space between her spirit and the omniscient.

When the audio had finished yesterday, she had played it again and she found her mind opened to the possibilities that life held for her. When Kamil had come home he was angry because she hadn't done the washing or cleaned the tiny flat, but she had borne his anger with a calm smile. She had lain awake beside him pondering the thoughts that God had awakened in her. Her desire to obey was strong but she wanted to be sure of His will. The pills opened her third eye to the transcendent, enabled her to see beyond petty human existence. She needed that clarity again if she was to be perfect in her submission.

Shahzia took three of the pills with a glass of water, gulping them down at the sink as soon as she had closed the door on the courier. Then, looking at the packet of fifteen, she took two more for good measure. She felt the stirrings of their power within her and knelt on the prayer rug, pulling the headset over her ears and turning on the audio that would take her back to God. She rocked backwards and forwards as she heard the words and felt the wings of the angels, al-Malaikah, beat the air around her. She had a purpose now, a way to use her anxiety to the glory of God and punish those who did not deserve His grace. The faces of little children in the classes at St Mary's swam in front of her, eyes wide with innocence but she knew they would be with God soon. She knew now what she needed to do with the package and the crescendo of the music complete with divine orders filled her ears as she unpacked the vest and put it on. She had to hurry if she was to be there for break-time when all the children would be in the yard.

ARKANE, London, England. 3.02pm

Elias Marietti waved Morgan and Jake into his office. His usually immaculate desk was cluttered with papers and the wall TV screen showed a news bulletin with the sound muted, repeatedly showing scenes of destruction with tiny body bags laid neatly in rows. Protests had started and fire-brand preachers were calling for revenge.

"It's started," said Marietti. "There have been another two incidents this morning in addition to the ones in New York and North London. A Christian has blown himself up at the Independence Mosque in Jakarta and a Jewish soldier opened fire on a bus full of Muslim children near Hebron."

"This is the escalation of the religious element, perhaps the reference to death by sword in the prophecy," Morgan said, concern on her face. "But this will only be the beginning if Thanatos intend to take out a quarter of the world. If it's being spread through the Zoebios direct network there's no knowing how fast it will escalate and what extremists it may reach or even create."

Jake checked his tablet computer which held the latest information from Martin Klein about the perpetrators of the violence.

"The patchy information we have on the bombers so far indicates symptoms of anxiety and depression so they would have been candidates for the Zoebios audio program. We don't have time to wait for the bureaucracy of background checks on these people but there isn't enough proof to link them to Zoebios as yet."

"I know Milan Noble is behind this," Morgan said, determination in her voice. "We just need to find the evidence."

"So we go to him," Jake said. "There's a fundraiser tonight in Paris for the Foundation for a Sustainable Population, the politically correct arm of twenty-first century eugenics."

Marietti nodded as his private line began to flash again.

"Go," he said. "You need to stop this and it's the only lead we have. The missing pages of the Devil's Bible will have to wait. Right now, you have to stop this escalating into a holy war."

CHAPTER 21

Musée du Louvre, Paris. France. 6.16pm

THE PLACE DU CARROUSEL in central Paris was filled with beautiful people, while paparazzi snapped away, capturing their elegant dresses and fine jewels. Waiting staff carried trays of champagne and canapés to the guests spilling out of a pavilion pitched by the largest of the glass pyramids. The transparent edifices provided a modern foil to the regal architecture of the most visited museum in the world. The security checks to enter the museum were thorough so there was a pre-party catering service for the VIPs who queued in designer dresses, fur and diamonds. Jake watched Morgan skillfully swipe a glass of champagne from a waiter as he passed. She sipped it as Jake continued his briefing, already despairing of her.

"I don't think you're taking this seriously enough and I'm worried about you. Won't you consider letting me be your chaperone?"

Morgan smiled, taking a longer sip of the bubbles.

"No way. You agreed I would take point on this mission, so don't be backing out now. Besides, I'm here to find out more about Milan and you'll just spoil my personal approach."

Jake ignored her flirtatious smile.

"I'm not playing games. This place is a security nightmare

and it will be hard for me to get to you if you're in trouble."

"It's a fundraiser and there are hundreds of people here," Morgan replied. "He's not likely to try anything, is he? Not under the noses of all these glitterati. Besides, we do want him to pay attention to me. That was the whole point of this get-up."

She pointed at herself, a gold and garnet cross around her neck catching the evening sun. She had received it by courier this morning from Milan Noble with a brief note, thanking her for an expert tour of the relic exhibition. The cross was in a similar style to the one he had pointed out in the gallery. Despite the haste of their departure Martin Klein had modified it into a tracking device and also embedded a USB key in it that would enable him to hack any system Morgan plugged it into.

Jake couldn't help but glance at Morgan again, although he'd been trying to keep his eyes elsewhere since they'd left the houseboat. She wore a crimson flamenco style dress with plunging neckline and high spiked heels. The dress accentuated her slight curves and was slit open up one thigh. It left everything he wanted to the imagination. Her dark curls were mostly loose and she had pinned a garnet jewel in her hair to match the necklace. The deep scarlet suited her Mediterranean color. Her skin was darker after the summer months and the tan highlighted her cobalt blue eyes, the violet slash in her right eye darkening at Jake's intense gaze.

"You look good, " he said, flushing slightly. Morgan raised an eyebrow at his understatement. "Honestly, I wouldn't let you out in public, but the Director wants to know what's going on. You still need to be careful though."

Jake reluctantly agreed to stay in the crowd, observing and in contact with the backup team who were covertly hidden in a houseboat on the Seine nearby. Morgan pointed over his shoulder with her champagne glass.

"Now that's what I call a car."

Many in the crowd turned to watch as a fiery red sports car swung into the square and pulled up in front of the carpet leading to the pyramid. Jake whistled low.

"The man definitely has taste. That's a Joss JP1 super-car. Gorgeous."

"And good to see he likes red," Morgan said. "Now it's time for you to go socialize elsewhere. We can't be seen together. I'll be in contact later tonight, but give me some space Jake, I mean it. You've got me covered."

She touched the tracker hidden in the necklace. Jake nodded and melted into the crowd, turning briefly to watch Milan Noble stepping out of the car to the applause of the waiting crowd. He was alone and wearing classic black tie. The tuxedo was fitted to his slim hips and his jacket was open, a more casual look. He waved to the crowd but seemed almost embarrassed at the attention. Jake stared at Milan, wondering what secrets he hid behind that incredibly refined exterior. Through the crowd, he noted painfully that Morgan's eyes shone as she also looked at the man, her applause joining the others around her. Jake supposed the guy did look a little like James Bond and the car was definitely a lady killer. He bridled a little at being relegated to babysitting but he didn't mind too much as he got to watch Morgan all evening. In that dress, it would be a pleasure.

Morgan eventually made it down the elevators into the main atrium of the Musée du Louvre. It was light and airy, open to the pyramidal sky above. Diamond shaped panes let in the last of the evening sun which crept into the corners of the space. The evening's official function would be held in the sheltered sculpture courtyard of the Richelieu wing, but the guests had time to wander through some of the exhibits on their way. Morgan noticed a number of interested male guests who saw that she was unaccompanied so she pretended to be looking for someone specific and headed towards the courtyard. She glimpsed Jake cornered by a young woman, a peach satin sheath clinging to her dangerous curves. He was looking in her direction but didn't catch her eye, deliberately she thought. A fast pang of annoyance flashed through her, and she was surprised. Jake did look good but then a tux suited practically any man and tonight, her target was Milan Noble, who certainly looked stunning in his.

Morgan walked up the wide stairwell, mingling with the guests as they slowly made their way through the museum, distracted by the priceless objects. The Louvre was an over-whelming place, so crammed with art that every painting began to look the same after a while. Morgan knew the key to these great museums was to pick an interesting piece and spend longer with it, focusing and appreciating its beauty. En route to the courtyard she stopped before Canova's Psyche Revived by Cupid's Kiss. The white marble looked soft to the touch. The folds of Psyche's dress, the curves of her arms, the feathers on Cupid's wings, all fluid and supple. Morgan loved sculpture and it moved her far more than painting. She wanted to run her fingers over the smooth hip, to trace the outline of Cupid's lips. A voice interrupted her reverie.

"Mesdames et messieurs, bienvenue au Musée du Louvre. Welcome to the Louvre, ladies and gentlemen."

Morgan could hear polite applause as people made their way up into the courtyard and she headed in that direc-tion with a group of guests. The area was open to the sky, protected by glass panes that allowed a buttery light to filter down, touching the guests and statues with gold. There were small trees set with low marble benches and sculptures dotted around the multi-level terraces. It was reminiscent of Narnia, a kingdom of stone where the Gods had been frozen in time.

The Master of Ceremonies tapped on the microphone.

"We are here tonight to raise money for the Foundation for a Sustainable Population and our lead patron, Milan Noble from Zoebios, will be speaking to us shortly. He has also donated some amazing prizes for the auction later, so please raise your glasses and join me in a toast. To a sparkling evening."

Morgan raised her glass with the crowd as Milan Noble took the stage. He stood like a lord over them, looking down from a raised dais near a statue of reclining Zeus holding a thunderbolt. His face was impassioned as he spoke.

"Friends, it is evident that we are reaching a critical point in humanity's journey. We must begin to make sacrifices for the greater good, for never before have we been so threatened by our own choices, and every individual must take responsibility for the planet's future. Zoebios aims to bring greater health and education to the world's people, but at the same time, we must reduce the number of our species. We cannot continue at this rate of growth and we are well past the point of sustainable population. Now is the time to change our future."

Morgan noted that he was an excellent speaker, making eye contact with many in the audience. She felt him look at her several times and then pass on. He was practiced at the art of working a crowd, but then he was the face and voice of his own organization, clearly experienced at persuasive performance and the manipulation of public opinion. She made her way to the side of the room near to the statues of the four seasons where she would stand out in her scarlet dress. It was important not to chase him for he was a man who could have anyone and anything so she must be just out of his reach, seemingly uninterested.

Milan finished his speech with another toast, the room effervescent with enthusiastic applause. As he stepped down from the dais, Milan was crowded by people pressing him with donations. Women wanted just that little bit of personal attention and the men were determined to shake his hand out of respect for his business prowess. But Morgan could see he was clearly moving in her direction through the crowd and she turned to study the statues as he approached.

"Again we meet in front of ancient and beautiful objects, Dr Sierra."

His voice was flirtatious as Morgan turned back to face him.

"But thankfully these are not quite so macabre. It was an interesting speech. You're quite the orator."

Milan smiled. "I see you're wearing my gift." He reached out and touched the garnet cross gently, his fingers near to her breast. Milan lent closer to her ear.

"I hate these events. I prefer my socializing to be more … intimate." He brushed a stray curl away from her face and Morgan realized she probably didn't need to try too hard to get him away from this crowd. She took a step back for it was too early to acquiesce.

"But these people all came to see you," she said. "Surely you don't want to disappoint them?"

"You're right, I must make my rounds." His regret was obvious. "But perhaps you would wait for me and we could go somewhere more private after the party? I'd love to tell you more about the plans Zoebios has for the future. I think you'll be most interested."

"Perhaps," Morgan said, looking around at the crowd, trying not to appear eager. "If I'm still here later."

Milan smiled at her coy reticence and strode back into the throng, immediately surrounded by supporters wanting a word.

As the evening progressed, Morgan was determined not to seek Milan out again, but it was a fine balance between ignoring him and trying to make sure he didn't disappear with anyone else. She needed to be sure it was her that he left with. If she could just get access to one of his private terminals, they might find the evidence they needed to link him to Thanatos and shut down the audio programs.

She flitted between the groups of donors, engaging in sparkling conversation with as many eligible men as she could before moving on when they became just a little too interested. Occasionally she spotted Jake through the crowd where he seemed to be paying special attention to the lady in the peach dress. Morgan was sure to always keep Milan within sight and be certain he knew where she was too. Their movements became a dance of courtship, an ever decreasing circle engineered to ensure they ended up together.

It was getting late and people were finally starting to leave. As Milan helped the Foundation seniority with farewells, Morgan caught his eye and indicated an arched doorway to her right, assuming he would follow when he could get away. A nearby waiter offered her another drink. She took one gratefully and stepped into the next room, away from the crowd at last. She took a long draught, in need of some courage since this femme fatale business was hardly her usual persona. She just hoped she could take it far enough to get the access they needed. Martin had been unable to hack into the deepest levels of Zoebios, so this was their only way in.

The room she entered was a long gallery, cramped with glass cases and dominated by a tall basalt pillar. Morgan recognized it as the Law Code of Hammurabi from the Mesopotamian court in Babylon, dated to the eighteenth century BC. She went to examine it more closely, expecting Milan to be a little longer. It was the most important legal compendium of the ancient near east, drafted earlier than the biblical laws. The text was cuneiform, containing the history of Hammurabi as well as legal judgments and a lyrical epilogue. She reached out to stroke the ancient surface, giving in to the sensation of wanting to connect with the past.

There was the sound of a step in the corridor and she pulled back, turning to face the doorway, expecting to see Milan. Instead, a security guard walked in.

"Are you fine Madame?" the man enquired.

"Yes, of course, thank you. I was just looking at the stele."

Morgan took another long sip of the champagne to hide her nerves, the glass almost empty now. The security guard came to stand next to her at the pillar.

"It is magnificent, isn't it," he said. "Many tourists walk straight past it. Perhaps they don't understand the unique insight it gives into the ancient culture that had such an impact on early civilization."

As the man spoke, Morgan began to feel dizzy. It wasn't alcohol, she hadn't drunk that much. The man came closer and clutched her arm. She couldn't speak, her tongue had grown thick and heavy in her mouth and the strength went from her legs.

"It's alright, Madame, just lean on me. Relax now."

In a haze of fear, Morgan realized she had been drugged. As she collapsed into the arms of the security guard, her last thought was of Jake, willing him to find her.

CHAPTER 22

Louvre, Paris, France. 11.15pm

SOMETIMES IT WAS NECESSARY to change the plan mid way through an operation. That was the nature of warfare, of espionage and Jake kept colleagues at a distance, preferring to be called aloof than to suffer loss as keenly as he had once before. But these defense mechanisms shattered when he realized that Morgan was gone. He walked down yet another corridor of the Louvre Palace, knowing even as he did so that he wouldn't find her in this maze of culture. He stopped in front of a striking painting by Delaroche. A young woman in white lay as if sleeping in calm water, her pale face lit by moonlight and the gold of a halo. Her hands were tightly bound with a leather strap and above her a dark figure loomed, looking down on his victim. A portrait of the aftermath of violence, Jake thought, seeing Morgan's face in the water. He turned away, his stomach clenching. It was time to get some help.

Martin Klein picked up on the first ring.

"Jake, what's happened? Morgan's gone dark."

Even in his concern, Jake smiled at the efficiency of his friend. He knew he had a good team behind him and hope kindled as he explained.

"We were separated in the crowd as the evening ended. I

could see her scarlet dress on the other side of the reception hall but I had to be sociable in order to maintain cover and turned away for a minute. Only a minute Martin…"

"I know Jake, it's OK. We'll find her. What then?"

"People were starting to leave and then suddenly she wasn't there. I've done a full sweep of the reception area now everyone has left. The Museum staff let me interview the security team once they found out I was on assignment. But there's no way I can look through the whole of the Louvre and surrounding buildings. It would take weeks, there are hidden passageways everywhere."

"Did she go with Milan Noble? After all, that was the point of the evening?" Martin asked.

"She certainly spent a lot of time talking with him." Jake remembered the way Morgan had looked at the man, touched his arm, laughed with him. Her hair had caught the light and drowned it in dark waves. He shook his head. "But she didn't leave with him. I didn't speak with him either as I didn't want to blow my cover, but he was one of the party saying goodbye to the donors and he left alone."

"He must have a team then or maybe it's someone else. What about security cameras?"

"They're claiming I can't view them until the morning so I need your help, Martin."

"Already on it. Give me ten minutes."

"OK, I'll head back to the houseboat and call you back." Jake was confident that Martin would find something. He was a virtuoso of code and would hack the Louvre from one of his special terminals, independent of other ARKANE equipment so it couldn't be traced or hacked back.

Jake left the Louvre and walked along the embankment path by the Seine. The Paris night would have been beautiful if Morgan had been by his side. He thought again of that scarlet dress and how earlier he had helped her climb out of the boat, holding her hand for the first time since the dying flames of Pentecost. He had been so conscious of her touch but it was brief and she had let go as soon as she was on the sidewalk.

The houseboat was moored under the Pont des Arts, where couples left padlocks with their names on to lock their passion into the city of love. He could see the Île de la Cité, green trees dripping over mottled grey walls and Notre Dame lit from below, a beacon of faith that Jake just didn't find inspirational tonight. He knocked on the hatch of the houseboat and heard the sound of the lock being drawn back. A concerned face looked out. Jean Pierre Moreau stood back to let Jake inside.

"Where's Morgan? I was going to come and find you. I've been going crazy."

"You and me both, JP. What time did her tracker go dark?"

"It was six minutes before you radioed to say she'd gone. Look at the logs."

Jean Pierre indicated the tiny computer station they had installed in the houseboat. The mission had only called for a small local contingent and JP had worked with Jake before. The two were fast friends. An empty wine bottle still stood on the table from their dinner last night, strangely out of place with Morgan missing.

"The trace disappears at the Jardin du Luxembourg."

Jean Pierre nodded. "So she's in a car. It's too far to make it there by foot in that time. It must mean she's being held in south Paris or at least heading south."

A light pulsed on the console. Jake clicked to answer the incoming call from ARKANE.

"Spooky, what do you have?"

Martin's fond nickname was due to his uncanny ability to find nuggets of information in an infinity of data. He never failed to deliver even if it took him years to do so.

"I'm sending the raw footage of that time period over

now Jake. You can click between the windows to see the various camera angles, but there's no sound."

The streaming video popped up in another window and Jake saw the party he had been at only hours before. The quality of the picture was excellent. From one camera angle, he could see Morgan talking to Milan Noble by a statue in the corner. She smiled up at him.

"Fast forward, this is too early," Jake said, not wanting to see her flirtatious manner with the man. The footage sped forward. Milan moved away to talk to donors while Morgan walked around the gallery talking to various people but always moving on. Then she stopped and indicated towards another room before heading through an arched doorway, taking a glass of champagne from a waiter on the way in.

"Stop it there Martin. Is there a view from the room she's about to enter?"

"That's the code of Hammurabi room so yes, there's a feed."

The screen changed to a smaller room, cluttered with display cases that obscured angles. Morgan walked in alone, holding the glass tightly as if it was an anchor for her sanity.

"Elle est magnifique," JP whispered. Jake said nothing but watched as she went to stand in front of the basalt pillar. She reached out to touch it, then she pulled her hand away sharply and looked towards the entrance she had just come through.

"She's heard something."

Jake watched as Morgan's face relaxed. A security guard came in and she played the part of the interested tourist. He came to stand next to her and she took a larger swig of the bubbles. Then she reached out, unsteady on her feet, her face confused. The guard held her elbow to support her and then put his arm around her waist as she slumped against him. He looked around to see if anyone had seen, then spoke into his radio.

"The champagne. She was drugged." Jake banged his fist down onto the table and watched as another guard came in and together they half carried the unconscious Morgan away from the gathering and out another door. "Bastards. They weren't official security guards either, at least not from the detail that I interviewed afterwards."

JP leant forward.

"Are there any more feeds, Martin? Where did they take her next?"

"The cameras show them outside entering a small black Fiat. I'm looking for CCTV now to track where it went next."

Jake was pacing up and down as far as he could on the tiny houseboat floor.

"What do you think, JP. Was it Noble? He seemed mightily interested in her."

Jean-Pierre shrugged.

"She's a beautiful woman and I wouldn't blame him for being interested. But he didn't pour the drink and we still aren't sure that he's involved in any of this. I don't think he has to drug the women he's interested in either. I mean the guy has looks, money, power. Why go to those lengths?"

"My gut says he has her, and that's all we have right now. Martin, I need you to go deeper with Milan. We haven't broken the data on his past yet, but now I need to know."

"I've started the pattern algorithms but that will take time. We already have all the superficial information, the publicly available stuff." Martin paused."Wait. It looks like the car is at Hôpital La Rochefoucauld. If you head down there, I'll start digging further. We'll find her, I know it."

Jake sat down heavily. Just for a moment he needed stability beneath him. He felt JP's hand on his shoulder.

"Mon ami, don't worry just yet. They want her for a reason, whoever they are. They will keep her alive."

Jake looked up at his friend.

"But for what reason? Why could they possibly need her?"

CHAPTER 23

Catacombs, Paris, France. 11.50pm

MORGAN WOKE IN PITCH darkness, shivering with the cold, and tried to orientate herself. She was still wearing the flamenco dress from the party and the earth was damp beneath her bare arms. Her shoes and bag were gone. She touched the cross around her neck. At least she still had that. She sat up slowly, her head spinning, bracing herself with both arms on the floor until the dizziness subsided. Her fingers dug into the dirt. It smelled like peat, earthy and pleasant. It was soft from the damp and she could hear the dull thwack of water dripping from a low ceiling nearby. Morgan listened intently. In the distance, she could hear voices muted by the heavy air.

She stretched out and shuffled to the right, sweeping her arms in a wide circle before her. Her fingers brushed a cold wall and she moved to face it in the dark, tracing the ridged surface. It felt hard like concrete but the texture was unusual, a repeating pattern of knobs and notches with smooth patches between. She used the wall to pull herself up and then felt along the top of it. There was a gap so she reached an arm out, touching a pile of debris that lay on top, spiky in parts, with irregular shapes and some loose pieces. Picking one up, Morgan ran her other hand over the object. As she felt its smooth length with a ball on one end and scalloped notches on the other, she realized it was a human femur. Fighting the urge to drop it, she focused on the cool of the bone she held. After all, the dead couldn't hurt her. The dead didn't drug her and leave her here in the cold and this femur could be a weapon, a makeshift baseball bat.

Voices became clearer in the passage and she could see a faint light approaching. Morgan sank to the floor, this time with the femur tucked beneath her. She faced the oncoming light with eyes closed and focused on the voices. A torch shone in her face. She didn't react.

"She's still out."

"We'll have to wake her soon, as the boss is coming down after the party. Did you give her too much sedative?"

"No, I swear, I just followed the directions on the bottle."

"Genius," the man snorted. "Right then, we're meant to treat her nice so we'll have to wake her gently. I can think of more interesting things to do, but that's orders for now."

Morgan sensed he was bending down towards her and in that moment, she thrust herself up from the floor, whipping the femur around and catching the man square on the side of his face. It was a powerful blow but she couldn't put full force behind it from that angle. Nevertheless he grunted and fell sideways. As the torch dropped to the floor, Morgan caught a glimpse of the piles of bones that made up the walls of the tunnel. The man began to right himself and she used the femur again, this time like a battering ram into his lower belly. He doubled over and sank to the floor, winded and gesturing to the other man to do something but he didn't look keen to engage. Morgan turned and grinned, slapping the femur bone into her other hand, taunting him.

"Come on then, what are you waiting for? You want to treat me nicely?"

"Why can't you just come with us? We're not going to hurt you, we just need you to see the boss."

He was almost pleading with her, one eye on his friend who was seconds from recovering. Morgan knew she had little time, so she feinted left and as the second man bent to catch her she ducked past him in the narrow corridor. As she went under his arm, she jabbed the femur hard into his kidney and ran down the passageway into the dark. Finding an alcove, she bent her body into it, pressing against the bony wall. She heard them cursing and swearing, then the first man shouted.

"We're going to find you, Dr Sierra. It's only a matter of time. There are kilometers of tunnels down here. You sit tight now. We'll be back."

As their footsteps faded up the passageway, Morgan's heart rate slowed as the adrenalin of the fight passed. They hadn't been prepared for her but they would be next time and the chill was starting to penetrate her bones. This dress had been perfect for the Louvre party but was hardly protection against the cold down here. With bare feet and no way of warming herself, she would soon be affected by the cold and they would catch her. She had to find a way out.

In the glimpse she'd had of the walls in the torchlight, she realized she must be in the catacombs, deep below the fourteenth arrondissement in Paris. She had been here once, years ago, when visiting the Faculté Libre de Théologie Protestante de Paris, on nearby Boulevard Arago. One of the pastors had given her a tour of this Empire of the Dead. He had told her that the catacombs contained nearly six million skeletons, the bodies moved from public cemeteries at the end of the eighteenth century to stop the spread of disease. Here in the cool darkness, Morgan didn't feel any sense of dread or foreboding, yet she knew the bones were piled here in corridors stretching for kilometers underground. Morgan had seen pictures of the bodies brought here on carts, only ever at night in order to save the people of Paris from the disturbance. There had been rumors of grave-robbers, the dead rising as zombies and the hand of Satan, but there was a different feeling to the malevolence of the Palermo crypt. These skeletons were witnesses to life but they had passed on. They were architecture now, forgotten individuals but together they became a fitting memorial for the deaths of unknown millions in the Black Death and the poorhouses of Paris.

Water dripped onto Morgan's shoulder, the freezing chill running down her back. She shivered. Enough dwelling on the past, she thought, it was time to get out of here. Feeling her way along the wall, she started to walk, her fingers lightly touching the arrangement of skulls and femurs as she went. A light glowed up ahead as she turned a corner. She flattened against the wall again, but there was no sound and so she walked towards it on quiet feet. The light permeated the tunnel and soon she could see the walls clearly. A multitude of bodies locked together in death, fitting perfectly like one enormous body with skulls in decorative arches and rows that broke up the pattern. Some had holes in them, some were cracked and others smooth. All had the dull patina of age and they seemed to be cemented together, as if they had sunk into each other after years of standing here, sentinels to death. Morgan saw that the light came from a lamp lit in an alcove and she rounded the corner with the femur held high. Padding forward on bare feet, tiny stones pricking her soles, she moved towards the lamp.

"It's the Sepulcher Lamp," a voice came from around the corner and Milan Noble stepped from behind a wall of bones. She started towards him, but two men appeared from behind him. Morgan turned to run back into the dark but the two men who had captured her were walking towards her from that direction. She was trapped so she threw down the femur and turned to face him. It seemed best to play Milan's game, since for now, she was outnumbered.

"It watches over the souls of the millions that reside here

in the Catacombs," he said.

"And who watches over your soul?" Morgan answered.

Milan laughed, a deep rumble that was dampened by the dead earth. He undid his bow tie and shrugged off his tuxedo jacket.

"Oh Morgan, I wanted you to see what I'm building here. This whole thing wasn't meant to hurt you, but I needed to be sure we weren't followed. I know you're working with ARKANE, so I needed to extract you carefully. You can't stop the plan now, but there's something I wanted you to see, and maybe even be part of. You seemed quite keen to get to know me earlier."

Milan offered her his jacket in a gesture of peace. She walked towards him in her bare feet, aware that her dress was now damp and marked with dirt, but she was still an attractive woman and she could use that. Morgan saw his eyes drop to her breasts, nipples hard in the cold air of the buried tunnels. In the half light, with an amber glow from the flickering lamp, he was leonine in looks, a man in his prime. What did he want with her? She turned and accepted his jacket, pulling the fine wool around her, grateful for the warmth.

"I'm sorry for the way you've been treated," he said. "But it seems you can handle my men by yourself." He shrugged in the direction of the now sheepish men who had let her escape. "If you'll walk with me now, I'll show you what we're hiding down here. Few have seen this Morgan, but I feel that you particularly will appreciate what I am creating. It's not just about destruction but also about new life for those who will remain."

Milan touched the small of her back and guided her up the tunnel. Morgan's mind was racing as she walked with him, her fingers delving into the pockets of his jacket in case there was anything that could help her. The tracker wouldn't work this far underground so how was she going to get word to Jake of where she was? And what did Milan have down here in this underworld of bones? She couldn't help but be curious.

The sepia light of the catacombs made it as unending dusk as Milan steered Morgan along the maze of tunnels. The guards behind now had their guns out at the ready and Morgan knew they wouldn't let her get away again. At the end of a darkened corridor, Milan flicked a switch hidden behind a pile of skulls and a door opened to reveal a bright, white box room.

"Now you will see what I have been working towards behind the clinical facade of Zoebios. Come," Milan said, stepping inside. Morgan followed him in and found the room was an elevator with retinal scan and voice recognition protection. The guards entered behind them as Milan activated the controls.

"So what is this place?" Morgan asked, "and why isn't it part of the official Zoebios infrastructure?"

"This is Sector C, where we work on secret projects that aren't officially sanctioned, on the fringe of what would be considered acceptable to the global health market." Milan raised an eyebrow at her. "Actually, some of it would be deemed utterly unacceptable, hence the secrecy of it all."

His words filled Morgan with unease. How could he be taking her somewhere so secret if he meant to let her go again?

The door opened onto the atrium of what looked like a high-end medical facility and Milan led her into a further maze of clinical white corridors. Armed guards were stationed outside every room, faces stony, staring straight ahead as they passed. Clearly any problems would be dealt with swiftly and with violence. Opaque glass doors inscribed with the Zoebios logo led to patient rooms and Milan stopped at a wall sized glass window. Behind the barrier, a team of scientists worked in protective clothing on immaculate chrome and silver equipment. There was a hum of controlled activity; the sound of progress or perhaps the sound of descent into scientific insanity.

"This is what I wanted you to see," Milan said with a triumphant tone.

"OK," said Morgan. "But you might have to explain what's going on. My biological science is a little rusty."

Milan smiled.

"Of course, you know that Zoebios is the foremost company in family planning, birth and neonatal health and you know of my interest in population control. This is the logical extension of those interests, as we are genetically modifying human embryos."

"That's not new though, right?" asked Morgan. "Wasn't that done a few years ago?"

"Yes, in a very basic sense but here we are taking it much further. For a start, embryos have actually been implanted in human mothers and the babies will soon be viable, although we are still testing the various batches."

Morgan stared at him in horror.

"What do you mean 'soon be'? And what's a batch?"

Milan waved her concerns aside.

"No matter, but I thought you'd be particularly interested in the genetic material we have found in the cells from the religious relics. It's one of the test conditions for the embryos. We're experimenting with enhancing that material to make super-spiritual people and then removing it entirely to see if that creates atheists. It's only one of the variables of course; we're testing with many different conditions." He pointed to the lab. "Here we are designing the future of the human race."

"So this is basically eugenics," Morgan stated, her mind

playing back the conversation with Martin and Jake. It was as they had feared, there was another part of the Thanatos plan, but how far had Milan progressed down this path?

"The principles of eugenics are sound," he explained. "They've just been tarnished with the past. But we need to improve the human race, not dilute it with imbeciles, handicapped and the impure. We breed animals with these principles in mind, selecting the best ones to continue the line and slaughtering the rest. The same should be done with humans."

In that moment, Morgan knew that he must be behind the theft of the Devil's Bible and the suicide attacks. She wanted to goad him on. She needed to know it all and somehow she would get the information out and make it public. Somehow she would stop this madness.

Milan continued with his rant.

"People pay more attention to the breeding of their cats than they do to the breeding of the human population. Hitler was only criticized because he killed by race, but it's not race that matters. There is an underclass in every culture who contribute little worth to the furthering of the human species. These must be weeded out for the health of the rest. You know the world is under incredible pressure from over-population and we have caused the destruction of so much. The sea is poisoned, the fish are almost gone, new species become extinct every day and we are crammed into mega-cities where no one can breathe. People abuse their children and hurt loved ones. There aren't enough jobs. Poverty and violence persist across generations and it's not a pleasant world when there are seven billion mouths to feed. Think how much better it would be if we reduced the population by one quarter. One in four people gone for the sake of the greater good."

He walked up and down, seemingly agitated, then turned to Morgan in appeal.

"Let's face it, not everyone deserves to live. Imagine if we could rid the world of the worst quarter and raise better humans with enhanced capacity. That is my vision Morgan, that is my mission."

Milan's eyes were alight with fanaticism and his true self was revealed in that moment. The cool, smooth talking CEO was gone and in his place was a psychopath with the global power to recreate humanity in whatever image he wanted.

"Don't you see that humans are different to animals?" she pleaded. "We have free will, we can choose."

Milan spun towards her, grabbing her by the shoulders, almost shaking her in his ferocity.

"I disagree," he said passionately. "Humans are not different. We're herd animals, we obey the authority of others. We do as we're told. We work, sleep, fuck, watch TV and switch off. Most humans basically subsist for a miserable lifetime and then die. Why shouldn't those of us with more intelligence be superior? Why shouldn't we be the ones who choose who is allowed to procreate and who cannot pass their inferior genes to the next generation?"

Morgan pulled violently away from him, unable to stand his tirade. The nearby guards put their hands on their weapons at her sudden move.

"You have no right to do this," she shouted.

"But don't you think the wrong people have children now?" Milan continued. "Birth rates among educated societies are dropping as women find a life that doesn't involve being pregnant all the time. The people who should be producing the next crop of humans are not doing so. But the criminals, those on benefits, the poor, the stupid, the hyper-religious, the immigrants; they are having the bulk of the children. The world will be a better place with fewer people but it needs to be less of the wrong kind of people and more of the right. My mission is to make that happen, and with Zoebios spearheading global family planning, we can adjust the situation."

"But Zoebios is aimed at the health of mothers and children, isn't it?" Morgan asked, as the scope of his plan became clearer.

Milan laughed.

"Oh Morgan, how naïve. The centers are for education but also for sterilization and enhancement. Zoebios is enacting the ancient Spartan laws in order to save humanity from a threat that could send us all back to the stone age."

"The Spartans practiced infanticide of the weak. Is that what you're doing?"

"Come now, we have more sophistication than that. Time and technology have enabled us to start much earlier. We have systematized a selection of tests that women respond to when they first come to the clinics. Based on the answers, they are given a score and a drug batch is allocated. Those who are fit to continue the human race are given vitamins and vital supplements including brain boosting hormones for the baby. Those who fail are given the sterilization batch. Of course, the health nurses don't know what they're giving them but remarkably, they just do what they're told."

Morgan was aghast.

"But you're doing this without people's consent. It's not your place to decide who should have children and who should not."Milan stepped away from her, his eyes cold.

"I'm disappointed. I thought you were a scientist, someone who would appreciate the beauty of what I'm doing here. It won't be long until the world knows everything as the final stages are in place but it is too late to stop it now. You know I have the means to destroy a quarter of the world and now you know I can remake it again in a much better way. Surely you want to join me and be part of the future? I need eggs from women like you for the program, strong genetic material that will be beneficial for the new world."

Morgan's temper exploded and she spat at him through clenched teeth.

"I would never be part of this. It's an abomination."

He took out a handkerchief and wiped his face lazily, a smile playing about his lips. Her response seemed just what he wanted to see, evidence of her strength of character.

"Earlier this evening, you were almost in my arms by choice. You know I'm genetically superior, why so shy now?"

Morgan shook her head violently.

"You disgust me."

Sensing the danger she was now in, she looked around to see three of the guards closing in on her, two with meaty hands spread wide and one with a taser. Behind them stood a man in a white coat with a syringe.

"You have nowhere to run," Milan said. "I had hoped you would join me by choice, but no matter, I will have you anyway."

Morgan launched herself at Milan with fist clenched. She managed to connect a fierce hammer strike before being dragged off him by the guards. She grunted as she hit the ground and was pinned face down. She struggled but their grip was unyielding and she felt the prick of the needle on her arm. The lights dimmed and the sensation of falling faded to black.

DAY 6

CHAPTER 24

Sector C, Paris, France. 5.16am

MORGAN WOKE FROM A nightmare of screaming skulls. A dull pain thumped through her brain. Her first thought was of Milan and his psychotic plan, her second of how to escape and stop him. She tried to sit up but found herself manacled to a hospital bed with little ability to move. At least she could still feel the weight of the gold cross around her neck for in some kind of hubris, Milan had left his personal mark on her and she could still be tracked if she could only get above ground. She moved her head slowly and looked around. There was a logo on the door, the Zoebios unfurling shoot of new life, so she was still in their facility. Through the opaque glass door she could see the movement of people in blue uniforms.

The door opened.

"Welcome to Zoebios. I'm Dr Harghada."

It was the man who had wielded the syringe. He stood incredibly straight as if a metal rod held him upright, his blue-black hair thick and perfectly styled.

"I'm not here by choice," Morgan replied. "But then you know that."

"No matter. You've been chosen by Milan and that's all the choice you have." The man smiled, a savage glint in his eye. "Usually, once the subject is under, she stays under. But Milan wanted something a little more personal for you. He wants you to see the farm before we put you back under for good."

Morgan's mind raced. At least she still had some time. She couldn't have been out for that long and she knew Jake would be searching for her. She yanked in frustration at the handcuffs that held her to the bed. Harghada laughed.

"Now, now. No need to be so aggressive. You have two choices. Come quietly to the farm and I'll show you what Milan wants you to be part of, then we can sedate you and you won't feel a thing. Or I can forcibly start the process now, with you awake and screaming. What's it to be?"

Morgan stopped struggling.

"I want to know what you're up to here," she said. "You won't get away with it. We know about the Devil's Bible, the suicide bombers."

"But there's so much more, Dr Sierra. The plan is far-reaching and stretches over generations. I'll show you, but I think we'll keep you manacled for now."

He called for an orderly and they forced Morgan into a wheelchair, her hands swiftly manacled to the frame. Harghada wheeled her out of the room and down a long hallway with rooms on either side, although she couldn't see in.

"What exactly do you do here?" she asked, counting on the Doctor's arrogance to explain what was going on.

"You know Thanatos will rid the world of the useless quarter, destroying those who are unproductive in society. Well, there is no point in the destruction unless you can reinvent the new. Zoebios is about life in all its fullness, the true ethics behind eugenics. We want to rid the world of the weak, the useless and keep the smart, the productive, the intelligent ones. Thankfully, after so long, the next phase is almost upon us."

"It's a huge and ambitious project," Morgan said, as if the plans were completely rational. "But what part am I meant to play?"

"You'll see in just a few moments."

Harghada swiped a card at the next door. They entered an air lock and compressed air blew over them, the scent of antiseptic heavy in the blast.

"This is just to make sure we're sterile. Now, you'll see the farm and your place with us."

The doors opened at the other end of the airlock and Harghada pushed Morgan out, wheels squeaking on the pristine floor. She gasped in horror at what she saw.

CHAPTER 25

Houseboat, Paris, France. 5.31am

JAKE RAN HIS HANDS through his hair, tugging it as he tried to think of some other way to find Morgan. He took another sip of cold coffee and reached behind JP to turn on the percolator again. They had been up all night trying to find where she could have been taken. Martin Klein was still working on the databases back in London and JP was scouring security camera footage trying to piece together the clues.

As the minutes ticked away, Jake was increasingly worried for Morgan's safety. The Hôpital La Rochefoucauld had proved a dead end; the car was found abandoned with no evidence inside. It had been parked outside the orbit of any cameras so the kidnappers could have swapped cars with no witnesses at that time of night. Jake's guilt weighed upon him. He had let jealousy override his natural caution. He couldn't bear watching Morgan flirting with Milan Noble so he'd given her too much space when he should have protected her. He banged his fist down on the table, frustration spilling over.

"We'll find her." JP put his hand on his friend's shoulder. "Martin's the best in the business and we've got a team mobilized. The moment we have a lead we'll be off." Jake sighed.

"Marietti's livid but he's sending the best to help us although he has enough on his plate with the spiraling religious violence. The public side of ARKANE is being called to press conferences to explain this sudden upsurge in religious fundamentalism."

JP shook his head.

"How little people know of what actually goes on behind the scenes."

"And better it stays that way."

The video phone chimed and Martin Klein appeared on the screen. Jake could see he wasn't the only one tearing his hair out over finding Morgan. He topped up his coffee cup with a fresh brew as Martin spoke.

"Milan Noble is a black box. It's like he appeared out of nowhere fifteen years ago with a lot of money and built this company from nothing. I've hacked as far as I can and I can't find anything in their systems relating to Thanatos. But I have found reference to a Sector C which isn't on the Zoebios official listings."

"That sounds like our only lead for now. Where's this Sector C? We can't go storming into Zoebios unless we know exactly where she is."

"I've been tracking Armen Harghada who seems to be a kind of clean-up man for Noble. He spoke to the press earlier this week about the tragic suicide of one of their top research scientists who jumped from the twenty-first floor. It just so happens that this scientist was responsible for the trials of the anxiety and depression audio programs. I tried tracking him instead of focusing on Milan as he must be heavily involved in Sector C."

Jake leaned towards the screen.

"OK, what have you found?"

"Harghada frequently enters a plain building on the Rue Dareau only a few blocks from the entrance to the Paris catacombs. It's quite near the Centre Hospitalier Sainte-

Anne where he has some kind of medical consultancy role, but that seems to be an honorary position of sorts. It certainly it doesn't justify the amount of time he's spent there recently and Harghada was seen going in there again early this morning. You'd better hurry, as his reputation is not a savory one."

"That's it. We're going in now," Jake said. "Get the order out JP, and we'll rendezvous with the team there."

"There's one more thing," Martin said. "Milan Noble held another scheduled press conference this morning and there was a prominent bruise on his cheekbone which he declined to answer questions about."

Jake grinned at him over the video connection, a strange kind of pride welling up inside him.

"That's our girl."

CHAPTER 26

Sector C, Paris, France.

THE WAREHOUSE SIZED ROOM was packed with rows of beds and monitoring equipment. Morgan could see a woman in each bed, masked and sedated as nurses patrolled the machines, checking the bleeping monitors. Each woman was pregnant, some showing only a little and others with huge bellies that must be almost full term. In the middle of the space was a round guard station where uniformed men sat watching the hospital floor, guns at their hips.

"What are you doing here?" she gasped. "Who are these women?"

"The farm is being used as the basis for our eugenic research." Pride was evident in Harghada's voice. "We have been testing drugs for cognitive enhancement and I think we have perfected it in the latest batch. The previous batches had to be terminated but so far this crop is working out fine."

"This crop?" Morgan said, aghast.

"We have to think in terms of a harvest of perfect genetic specimens. These are all grown from variations of Milan's sperm, and of course, you'll be joining them. We always need smart women as carriers and it's easier to control like this. These children will be born smarter and more able than others. It's the dream of eugenics made reality."

Harghada wheeled Morgan through the rows of hospital beds. She looked into the impassive faces of the women. They looked peaceful but she wondered if they were screaming inside their trapped bodies.

"How did you find them all?" she asked, estimating that there were nearly 100 women in various stages of pregnancy.

"Some of them came willingly. Many believe this world is not a great place anymore, that there are sacrifices needed for the greater good. These women were promised that their children would be as gods in the new world."

"But not all came willingly or I wouldn't be here," Morgan said darkly, as the wheelchair squeaked across the floor.

They progressed towards an operating theatre at the end of the room where nurses in gowns were prepping and cleaning equipment. As Morgan watched, a bed was wheeled out and a woman was put on the end of the far row. The woman's belly was flat but now presumably impregnated.

"Milan just takes a shine to some women. Like you. A smart woman, good breeding stock. Character. Definitely someone who should be saved and perfect for the farm. Don't worry my dear, we'll keep you and the baby safe here while the world rages outside these walls. After we've sedated you, we harvest your eggs, then fertilize them with Milan's sperm. We'll scan the embryos and implant the most viable with the best genetic code. You should be grateful to be chosen."

He patted her on the shoulder. It was all Morgan could do to restrain the screams that were welling up inside her. She scanned the room, calculating the amount of time she had before they reached the operating theatre, before they impregnated her, before she became just another body in this hell-farm. She had to keep him talking, keep him focused.

"I still don't understand your rush to proceed. Why not

just keep doing this in secret?"

"The twin aims of Thanatos and Zoebios have now combined with the retrieval of the Devil's Bible. We also know that the clinical research centers are beginning to be investigated and there's only a slim window before it all comes crashing down. People like you interfering mean we have to move the farm and the labs to a more secret location but we'll continue the research while a religious war explodes outside. Milan will release the final wave of the plan when he gets the last few pages of the Devil's Bible."

Harghada's face was lit up with the vision of this perfect future.

"But you've forgotten the human element," Morgan said.

"We have to make do with what we have, and you'll be part of it." Harghada's face darkened again and he wheeled her faster towards the operating theatre. "But you won't see the war to come, only the aftermath. That's if we keep this batch of course. I might have to make sure you don't survive to see your child born."

Ahead, Morgan could see a tight space between the hospital beds they would have to wheel through. It was her only chance.

Just before they hit the space, Morgan took a deep breath and with all her effort threw herself to one side, rocking the wheelchair over, tipping it and sliding under the bed closest to her. Harghada shouted in frustration. She heard the footsteps of others running to their position. She only had seconds before they got to her and she was still shackled to the wheelchair. She twisted around and with her teeth pulled a tiny pin out from under the skin on her left wrist. She palmed it just as the wheelchair was yanked back out from under the bed and she was dragged out with it.

"Stupid girl, how could you even think you'd get out of here?" Harghada was red-faced and flustered. Two orderlies helped him get her back into the wheelchair. "We need to get you sedated, there's no time for this. I'm sick of you. I don't care what Milan wants you for. To me, you're just another body, just another set of genetics for the farm. Bring her."

He stamped off and gestured for the orderlies to wheel her through to the operating area. Morgan could feel the pin sticking into her left palm, an old military trick that was uncomfortable at first but then became a kind of hair shirt, a penance that also had potential benefits. She only needed a few extra seconds to pick the lock on the handcuffs that held her there. But as they wheeled her forwards into the sterile area, Morgan could see Harghada putting on a gown and filling a syringe with something, so she didn't have long. She needed to stall for time.

"What if I submit willingly to the procedure?" she said. "You know the baby will develop better with an active mother."

The doctor's eyes flicked to hers over the syringe which he held ready to press into her arm.

"You're right of course. The babies would do better with mothers that weren't vegetables. But of course, I can't trust you."

He took a step towards her.

Suddenly an alarm sounded and lights began to flash. Harghada looked around in confusion. A security guard rushed into the room.

"The facility has been breached sir. You need to leave immediately."

Harghada put down the syringe and walked quickly to the main computer terminal.

"I need to replicate these files to the main server," he said to the man. "Then we must destroy the place. If this is discovered, Zoebios is over. Set the charges for ten minutes."

The guard nodded and ran off towards the central tower. The nurses left in a hurry. Harghada tapped away on the computer, his back to Morgan for a moment. With one hand, she gently maneuvered the pin until it rested on the side of the bed and then slotted it into the handcuff lock using her body as an anchor. She kept her eyes on Harghada, trying not to make any noticeable movements.

"Your friends, I presume," he said, looking up briefly. She froze. "I told Milan that involving you was a liability. This batch is wasted now but no matter. There are other labs, other facilities."

Morgan felt the lock click and she slipped her hand out, leaving it by her side as she surveyed the room for possible weapons. She needed her other hand free but in the seconds it would take to unlock it, he would be on her. She was fast, but not that fast.

The alarm turned into a countdown.

"Please evacuate. Eight minutes to detonation."

Harghada finished typing, folded his glasses into his pocket and picked up his coat.

"No doubt your friends will find you in time, but then you will all be blown to pieces along with these women. There's no time and you'll die trying to save them. Goodbye Morgan, see you in hell."

He walked out without looking back. Morgan quickly used the pin to pick the other handcuff, jumped out of the wheelchair and then went to the computer terminal. It was dead; she couldn't use it to reach Martin. She peeked around the curtain of the sterile area. The orderlies were fleeing the area and the guards were leaving the central station. She could see Harghada moving through the beds towards an exit no one else was using. Morgan dearly wanted to follow him and make him pay for what he was doing here, but he was right, she needed to stop the explosion first. These women and the lives they carried were her first priority.

A rattle of gunfire came from the main entrance to the warehouse room and the guards moved towards the noise, leaving the central area unguarded. The automated voice spoke again over the din of gunfire and shouting.

"Please evacuate. Seven minutes to detonation."

Morgan ran towards the abandoned guard station, weaving through the beds with their impassive occupants. She needed to get to a terminal and stop the explosion. It sounded like Jake was on his way but at this rate he wouldn't make it in time and they would both die here in the flames. A dark anger burned inside her as she thought of what Harghada had done. If she made it out, she would go after him next and he would pay for this abuse. Even as she acknowledged the presence of a supernatural evil in the world, she knew it was made flesh in people like him, who would do anything to further their perverted cause. She reached the station and ran into the dark entrance.

Jake and Jean-Pierre were pinned down by the entrance to the underground warehouse. The advance team had blown the airlock and they had streamed in, exchanging fire with security guards who were using the bodies on hospital beds as cover. The ARKANE team had stopped firing when they realized the beds contained sedated women but the guards continued to take pot-shots even as they retreated to the far exit.

"What is this place?" JP shouted above the noise of bullets ricocheting off the metal struts lining the corridor. "You think Morgan's here?"

Jake reloaded his gun as JP popped up for another couple of shots.

"We have to find out if she is, even if we have to search every one of those damn beds."

"Please evacuate. Six minutes to detonation."

The bullets abruptly stopped. Jake peered around the edge of the door and saw the last guards heading for the exit.

"They're leaving. We've got to stop the explosion," he said, sprinting for the central guard station.

Morgan ran up the stairs softly on the balls of her feet, concerned that there would still be guards within. She could hear a voice and a crackling radio ahead.

"Detonation is imminent sir. Lockdown is in progress. Permission to withdraw?"

The man's voice contained a note of tension, understandable given the circumstances. Six minutes wasn't really long to get out of the huge building.

"Permission denied," Harghada's voice replied, with a crackle of static. "You will stay in place to ensure the detonation happens as planned and prevent any access to the main terminal. You will be shot if you emerge."

The radio went dead and Morgan could hear the guard swearing in fury and frustration, torn between duty and the desire to save his own life. Taking advantage of his distraction and orienting herself towards his voice, Morgan ran into the room. He looked up and reached for his weapon but with a palm strike, she knocked it from his hand, followed with a hammer fist to his nose, breaking it with an audible crunch. He grunted with pain as he fell backwards clutching his face.

Morgan's close combat Krav Maga tactics were second nature now and her anger and hatred for Harghada filled her with a fury that she now took out on this man. She used the edge of the table to give her some height as she jumped to knee him in the solar-plexus, sending him winded to the floor. Grabbing the gun from where it had fallen, she threw herself at him and slammed the butt of the gun into his face. His arms came up in defense as he scrabbled to get away from her. She swiped his arm away and hit him with the gun again, putting all the force she had into the blow. Blood welled up from the man's wounds and Morgan raised her hand to hit him again.

Her wrist was caught from above. She whipped around, ready to strike and saw Jake, his palm out to placate her even as she broke from his grip.

"It's alright," he said. "Better not kill him, we might need him later."

Morgan breathed out, letting the tension briefly subside. She could see her own anger reflected in his burnt amber eyes.

"You're late," she said. JP laughed and moved forward to help her off the man.

"We got a little sidetracked but you clearly didn't need the help," he said.

"Please evacuate. Five minutes to detonation." The voice said again. Jake moved to the computer terminal.

"We need Martin on this," Morgan said, pulling the jeweled cross from around her neck. She clicked the middle garnet and a slim USB key popped out the bottom. Morgan plugged it into the terminal and they waited a few seconds. The light on the stick changed from red to green and a little video screen opened in the window. The face of Martin Klein was pixellated at first and then resolved into his eccentric smile.

"Morgan, you're OK."

"All good here, Martin, but right now we need you to work some magic and stop a countdown. This place is about to explode."

"I'll get right on it."

They could see him working away, fingers flashing across

the keyboard. He muttered and then disappeared from the screen before rushing back and tapping again furiously. Jake was systematically searching the office, trying to find some evidence linking the site to Zoebios that they could use in the case against Milan Noble.

"Please evacuate. Four minutes to detonation."

Martin didn't even raise his head at this latest impassive announcement. Morgan watched him and felt a curious sense of displacement because it was too late to get out now. A few hours later and she would have been one of these nameless women, sedated and used to grow a new generation of smart people. It seemed like a parallel life, one she didn't recognize but she felt as if she was saving herself by saving these women. And if it wasn't to be, if the explosion happened, then she felt a sense of completion at that possibility. She was drawn to death, hunted it even, as she chased the memory of Elian. To die in a rain of fire as he had done would be right and she would perhaps join him in an exploded heaven. But was there something to live for now?

She glanced over at Jake, hastily scanning through papers in a filing cabinet. He had come to find her again and she had seen the deep concern in his eyes. He would never speak of it but they were bound together in some way.

"Got it!" shouted Martin. "Sending the code now. It's an elegant design so I've written an elegant solution."

He pressed a button.

"Wait for it," he said, pushing his glasses up his nose and gazing at them on the screen.

They waited. Seconds passed.

"Please evacuate. Three minutes to detonation."

The voice over the loudspeaker announced yet again. Jake came over to the screen.

"Spooky, we don't have much time here. Skip the elegant code and just nail this bastard."

Martin flushed. Morgan knew he hated to disappoint.

"Sorry Jake, give me another minute."

"We don't have much more than that, my friend," Jake said.

He looked over at her, a question in his eyes and Morgan could see that he wanted to say something to her. Jake glanced at JP who was still questioning the prisoner and getting nowhere. He walked towards her, his eyes locked on hers.

"Trying again." Martin's voice came from the screen. Jake stopped midway across the room and the moment hung in the air, like smoke from distant gunfire. Then Martin exhaled, a whoosh of triumphant air.

"Detonation cancelled. Evacuation no longer necessary." The disembodied voice came over the loudspeaker. The moment passed. Jake turned and walked back to the screen.

"Get the team down here Martin. These women need immediate medical attention and we need to move quickly now."

"And we have to find those missing pages before Milan does," added Morgan. "It's the only thing stopping him from igniting all-out war."

DAY 7

CHAPTER 27

MORGAN STRODE PURPOSEFULLY DOWN the long corridor, past the well-lit workrooms of the ARKANE research departments towards the dark den that was Martin Klein's office. Her anger at Milan and Harghada burned even more fiercely now as the body count rose with increasing attacks by people who had suddenly turned into religious extremists. The rhetoric from all sides was escalating and with their methods about to be exposed, it would only be a short time before Thanatos executed their final plan in order to capitalize on the carnage. The missing ten pages of the Devil's Bible were the key for without them, Milan would not be able to embed and release the curse that would tip the bloodshed over into total destruction. He might have the book, but he didn't yet have the final words to fulfill the prophecy on the intended scale.

Marietti hadn't been able to dig up anything from the Vatican archivists on where the missing pages might be. Ben had hit a similar dead end, but the pages of the Devil's Bible she had glimpsed were seared onto Morgan's brain. When she had looked at the pages of the illuminated book in the Palermo crypt, Morgan had felt the stirrings of recognition. She had seen some of those images before; she just had to work out where. Martin's virtual library was the place to start.

Morgan arrived at Martin's door and knocked with a tentative hand, knowing that the eccentric genius didn't like to be disturbed. A second passed before the door was wrenched open. Martin was clearly in the middle of something as his rough-cut mop of blond hair was spiked where he had been tearing at it. The sleeves of his blue shirt were rolled up in precisely matching creases. He pushed his wire rimmed glasses up the bridge of his nose.

"Morgan, come in, come in," he said, standing back to let her into the chaos of his office. For someone so painstakingly neat in most ways, his office was evidence of a more disordered psyche. Morgan was pleased to find he seemed genuinely happy to see her, even without Jake.

"I'm working on the data downloaded from the terminal you were able to access," he said. "We're close to finding the other labs. The legal liaison are swinging into action, but they take so long to do anything. Not like you and Jake." He grinned.

"I need to use the pod, Martin. Jake said you wouldn't mind?"

She gestured at the stand up module in the corner of the office.

"I still haven't quite finished the alterations but if you don't mind the beta version, then please go ahead. It's quite intuitive, and of course, you know the Bodleian Library anyway."

Martin sat down and clicked on his laptop. The door slid open and Morgan stepped into the booth, the door sliding closed behind her. It was dark except for a tiny light that illuminated a headset complete with visor.

"I forgot to mention." Martin's voice came over a hidden microphone. "The sensors will read your body movements so just pull information from the shelves or page through the books. You're also on a rolling platform so you can walk through the physical space. You'll get the hang of it. Just leave the library when you've finished."

Morgan pulled on the helmet and incredibly the high domed ceiling of the Radcliffe Camera loomed above her, the top stacks in shadow. Sun streamed through the glass windows onto the wooden desks. Morgan felt like she was indeed back at Oxford researching her latest academic paper. Although the library was digitized, there was still serendipity in wandering the physical environment and seeing what else caught her eye. She walked towards one of the stacks. It was a strange sensation and she wobbled at first but soon stabilized.

"Can I help you?" a voice asked, and she turned to see a librarian in classic cardigan, brunette bun and glasses. She must be Martin's fantasy, as Morgan couldn't remember any of the librarians she knew being this stunning.

"I'm looking for art related to the Revelation of St John and more specifically, the four horsemen of the apocalypse," Morgan said. The librarian paused, then indicated the stacks behind her. The shelves where Morgan was standing now had hundreds of books about the apocalypse on them. She pulled one down, put it on the wooden lectern and opened it. To her surprise, the images popped up in front of her, floating in the air. She could touch them and flick through them, making the search much easier.

Morgan knew that the word apocalypse meant unveiling, an uncovering of secret knowledge about heavenly realms. It had become synonymous in popular consciousness with the Revelation of St John, the final book of the Bible which described the end times and the second coming of Christ. It was Revelation as an allegory of history, of things already fulfilled and a prediction of what is to come. The author John, possibly the same man as the gospel writer, wrote the book in exile on the Greek island of Patmos after he had survived the tortures of Domitian. There were those who claimed Revelation was a heresy, the visions of a lunatic, hallucinations brought on by fasting and dementia. To others it was the reality that lay as a foundation to all Christian belief. It had also spawned a great body of artistic work where Morgan hoped to find clues to the missing pages of the Devil's Bible.

She touched the virtual page. The first painting was by William Blake, an English poet and painter whose work delved into the spiritual realms. It showed Death on a Pale Horse leaping across the canvas. The figures were strong and muscled, Death as a powerful King with sword outstretched while the flames of Hell flickered beneath. Morgan brushed the image and more of Blake's paintings were arrayed before her. She gazed at the demonic brawn of The Great Red Dragon, curled horns and outstretched wings, about to devour the woman clothed with the sun. Blake saw the power of evil incarnate and portrayed him as thick limbed, unyielding, solidified muscle, not ethereal air. Morgan shivered for she felt the presence of a figure like this behind their current foe. The apocalypse was unveiling the true evil behind a global company that the material world saw as a life-giver. There was a marriage of opposites, as Morgan read from Blake's poem, 'In one evanescent moment, the Devil, boldly with eyes afire, clasps a shining angel in his embrace'. But Blake's images were nothing like the Devil's Bible; they were all his own visions.

She swiped the files away and pulled another virtual book from the shelves. This one contained paintings from John Martin, images of destruction in mezzotint, a manipulation of light and darkness. The apocalypse as holocaust and beatitude, heaven and hell combined. One caught her eye, so different from the rest of the annihilation portrayed in other paintings. Golden light suffused the image, the angel of revelation appearing from the sky above an open sea, almost a mirage. In the foreground, the silhouette of John, his hands raised to heaven, standing on a rocky outcrop receiving knowledge from On High. Morgan focused on the picture, sanity juxtaposed against the visions of massacre and ruination. But she sought darker art here and touched the screen again.

More paintings from John Martin appeared, no longer lit by heaven but more like the edge of hell, cracked open earth with fire spewing from it in Pandemonium, the Devil's court. Next to it, 'The Great Day of His Wrath' showed the world upended and folded over on itself, darkly thunderous apocalyptic majesty above an unholy abyss. The searing end to the world was dramatic but it wasn't what she sought.

The next image made her gasp. It was incredibly detailed and was unmistakably the same as the pictures of Revelation in the Devil's Bible that she had seen in the ossuary. It was a black and white print from a woodcut attributed to Albrecht Durer, dated 1498. Four horsemen rode across the scene as if into battle, trampling the fallen beneath the hooves of their wild horses. The Conquerer on the white horse wore a crown and carried a bow, arrow notched in place to slaughter all before him. War raised his sword to swipe the heads from the unfaithful while Famine was depicted as a rich man, weighing scales in his outstretched arm. In the foreground rode skeletal Death on the pale horse, pitchfork in hand, as the devil Hades devoured with fiery mouth below him. Billowing clouds of coming destruction completed the scene. This had to be copied from the Devil's Bible, but how had Durer seen the book?

Morgan delved further into the database to find more information about the life of the artist. The image was from a woodcut print, one of a series that Durer made in his workshop in Nuremberg, Germany, not far from the borders of the Czech Republic. It was from a series about Revelation, each image an intricate portrayal of the events of John's apocalypse. She pulled up another virtual window and compared the dates of where the Devil's Bible had been kept. Could Durer have been in the same place?

After some searching, Morgan found that the Devil's Bible had been at the monastery of Broumov in the Czech Republic between 1477 and 1593. As one of the largest medieval illuminated manuscripts, it would have been quite the tourist attraction. Durer had also spent four years between 1490 and 1494 roaming Europe in what was known as the 'wanderjahre', a time when artists went to learn from other craftsman in a parallel to the modern gap year. There were no detailed records of his travels but his apocalypse series was made soon after his return. Clearly what he saw on that trip affected him greatly. But did he take the pages, Morgan wondered?

She touched the image of the four horsemen and it grew in size so she could gaze into the eyes of death. Durer's prints were scattered around the world but the original woodblocks and related material were held in the Staatliche Kunsthalle Karlsruhe, an art museum in Germany. Morgan turned and walked up the stairs out of the library and into the bright Oxford day which dissolved in front of her as she left the virtual world. She and Jake needed to make another trip.

CHAPTER 28

Staatliche Kunsthalle, Karlsruhe, Germany. 5.06pm

AFTER SOME WRANGLING, MARIETTI had arranged
for Morgan and Jake to examine the original Durer woodblocks in situ at the State Gallery and they arrived just before
closing time when only a few tourists remained. The sculp-
tured facade of the gallery was flanked by perfectly coiffed
mini trees, the bright green a contrast against cool cream
stone as they walked up the front steps.

Morgan had been reading about Durer on the plane. It
seemed that he may not have made the woodblocks himself
but designed the images then handed them over for a
master craftsman to cut the blocks. Part of the wood had
been chipped away leaving raised sections for the ink. The
block was then used to print onto paper or other mediums
to form an edition of the design and could be used multiple
times. Indeed, Durer had released a number of editions of
the apocalypse prints which had brought him fame and
wealth in fifteenth century Europe. If they were to find clues
to the missing pages, it must be with the physical blocks
themselves.

At the security check, they were asked to give up their
weapons. Jake argued with the guards but they were persistent, and in the end, their guns were stowed in the lockbox

for later retrieval. Finally, they were shown into a study room by the Curator. On the table, fifteen woodblocks were laid out, a spotlight overhead giving the ink stained shapes an ebony sheen. Morgan was intoxicated to be so close to the work of a genius craftsman.

"You have some time now to examine the blocks and then I will return to answer your questions," the Curator said with a thick German accent. She turned at the door. "Please ensure you wear gloves at all times when handling the blocks. The security guard is just outside."

She walked out.

"This is pretty exciting," Morgan said. "How do you guys have access to such treasures as these?"

"One of Marietti's little tricks," Jake replied. "The job of Director is all about who you know and what secrets you can manipulate in order to gain admission to Europe's finest. Shall we?"

With mock gallantry, he waved Morgan towards the table. They pulled on their white gloves and started to examine the blocks.

"What exactly are we looking for?" Jake asked, his brows creased in concentration.

"If the missing pages were taken by Durer as inspiration for his apocalypse series, then he must have hidden them somewhere. Since these blocks bought him money and fame, perhaps they are the key to finding the pages themselves."

"This one is pretty grisly, but incredible detail." Jake pointed down at a block that showed John the apostle being boiled in a vat of oil, a man basting him with a ladle. Flames appeared to crackle under the cauldron and a jeering court looked on from turreted castles as the saint prayed for deliverance.

"Incredibly, John survived that to go on and write the book of Revelation," Morgan said.

Jake picked up the block and looked at it more closely.

"Perhaps there's some kind of hidden mechanism in the block itself? They're thick enough to hold a compartment."

Morgan scanned the table and found the four horsemen scene. It was more dramatic in physical form and the relief of the carving made Death and Hades almost leap from the block into the room with them.

"This is the one I'm interested in. Why did Durer draw this specifically from the book?"

With gentle hands, Morgan picked it up and turned it around against the light, looking for a hidden seam. There was a faint line that ran around the edge of the block but it had been rubbed with resin or a filler of some kind and could barely be seen.

"What do you think of this?" Morgan showed it to Jake. "Could there be something in here?"

He traced the seam with his finger.

"We'd have to split the block open to get inside. That would just slightly break all the rules of the agreement we're here under." He smiled at her, his corkscrew scar crinkling. "But it's not like we haven't destroyed things together before."

A flash of memory and Morgan was back in the Iranian church of Mary of Tabriz hacking away at an ancient mural to find one of the Pentecost stones. She laughed.

"Maybe there are some tools around here we could use."

Suddenly, they heard shouting in the hallway, then gunfire and screams.

"I guess Thanatos did the same research you did," Jake said. "We need to get out of here. Maybe they don't know exactly what they're looking for."

Morgan took the four horsemen block and they quietly ran out of the back door into another gallery behind the workroom. It was high ceilinged, hung with paintings from the great German artists with wooden benches arrayed so people could stop and lose themselves in the art. A darkly crafted fireplace was laid ready to heat the place in a freezing winter. Morgan and Jake ran the length of the room to a staircase, ducking in just before the door slammed open behind them. The sound of running feet could be heard resounding in the gallery as they started down the stairs.

Then there was silence behind them. Jake held up his hand and they both stopped, careful not to make a sound that would give away their position. A woman's voice spoke stridently into the quiet. She had a faint American accent but as someone who had learned English as a foreign language.

"I have the curator and five other hostages here. If you give yourselves up now and bring the block to me, they will go free. I will count to ten and then the curator dies if you're not here to take her place."

A muffled scream and then the thud of a weapon against flesh. Morgan immediately turned to run back up the stairs. Jake grabbed her wrist.

"This is bigger than just those people," he hissed. "We have to get the block away from here."

She pulled her hand from his grip.

"We put those people in danger, Jake. It's our duty, and you know that. We'll work something out. We always do."

Jake shook his head with resignation but followed her back up the stairs. Morgan walked into the gallery with her hands held up in submission, one clutching the horse-men woodblock. Jake followed close behind. A tall slender woman with copper curls tumbling around her shoulders stood surrounded by men in black, their weapons raised. Six people knelt on the gallery floor, hands behind their heads. The woman walked towards them, her spike heels clicking on the parquet floor. In tight red leather trousers and a sheer lace black top that covered her arms to the wrist, she oozed sexual confidence with an edge of unstable violence. A handgun was tucked in her belt.

"I'll take that." She plucked the woodblock from Morgan's hand.

"I'm Natasha El-Behery and you must be Jake Timber," she said, stopping in front of Jake. In her tall heels she was eye level with him. She rested her palms on his chest and then ran them slowly down to his waist, unbuckling his belt, holding his eyes the entire time. Morgan could hear Jake's breathing become rougher at her flirtation. Then she stopped.

"I think I'll save you for later." She turned and walked back down the gallery towards the hostages. "Hold them," she commanded and several of the men stepped in to restrain Jake and Morgan. Natasha pulled her gun, walked up behind the gallery curator and with one shot to the back of her neck, executed her.

"No," cried Morgan, straining against her captors as the body thumped to the floor and the other captives groaned and wept in fear. The stink of emptied bowels flooded the room. Natasha stepped to the next hostage.

"Please," said Morgan. "What do you want from us? Just leave them alone."

"I want the pages. Where are they?"

"I think they're in that woodblock," Morgan replied. "We didn't get far enough to be sure before you arrived."

Natasha tucked the gun back in her waistband and looked down at the block. She turned it over.

"Go and find some tools," she said to one of the men. Natasha placed the woodblock on one of the benches. She looked at Morgan. "You will open it and find the pages. I will kill another person every five minutes and if you're wrong, then they all die. I will not go back empty-handed."

"Did you take the Devil's Bible from us in Palermo?" Jake asked.

Twisting a lock of hair around her fingers, Natasha replied slowly.

"I should have come and taken it personally from you, then we might have had this little meeting earlier."

Morgan felt a flash of anger at Jake as he seemed trans-fixed by this woman. Could she seriously be jealous at a time like this? The man returned with several chisels and a hammer and one of the guards pushed Morgan forward to the bench.

"Five minutes." Natasha clicked a button on her watch. She raised her gun and fired imaginary bullets at the hostages. "Or bang, bang."

Morgan tried to calm her breathing and push the anger aside. Her hands were shaking. She could hear the labored breathing and quiet weeping of the hostages. Natasha's heels clicked backwards and forwards as she paced. Morgan smoothed the back of the woodblock, feeling the seams. Selecting one of the chisels, she began to tap at the slender crack, trying to coax it open. It wouldn't budge. She hit it harder, at an angle, trying to drive a wedge in the gap. It moved a little, demonstrating that there must be a cavity inside. It was agony to try to prize it open without damaging the block. Over five hundred years of history; it seemed sacrilegious to be breaking it open like a common object.

"One minute left," Natasha said, walking towards the hostages. "Now which one do I choose next?"

Her voice was almost a caress and in that second, Morgan's anger grew white hot. Nothing mattered except finishing this. Her eyes darted around looking for something to use. Next to the fireplace was an axe in a glass case. Morgan leapt for the axe and broke the glass with the woodcut. Natasha spun around, her weapon raised as the hostages screamed in terror. A guard fired at Morgan defensively, but Jake pushed him aside and the bullets went wide, thumping into the fireplace. Morgan threw the wooden block down and with a blow of the axe, split it open as Jake punched the guard and was dragged off him by another.

"Hold your fire. Silence." Natasha shouted into the chaos, authority ringing in her tone. She walked with gun outstretched to Morgan's side and held the snub-nosed weapon against her temple. Morgan's breathing was fast from the exertion and she closed her eyes waiting for the shot.

"Well, well. It seems Dr Sierra has found the pages," Natasha said.

Morgan looked down at the block. The axe was still embedded in it, but the crack had opened enough to show a sheaf of parchment folded tightly into a space inside. She looked over at Jake and saw his relief reflected her own. She had known he would act to protect her, trusting her partner even as she knew she had acted rashly. But it had paid off again. How many more chances did she have?

"Open it," Natasha said, standing further back out of direct reach.

Morgan bent and wrenched the handle of the axe out.

"Careful now. Throw that back to the fireplace."

Morgan did as she was asked, then prized the woodblock open, pulling the pages gently from their hiding place. They felt waxy, as if they had been coated with something to preserve them. She unfolded them and saw that the illuminated pages clearly matched the Devil's Bible. Words swirled on the pages. Morgan tried to read some of them, the Latin ancient and stilted, hard to understand, but they were mesmerizing, intoxicating just to look at. Time seemed to slow and Morgan wanted to sink into them, to savor the words on her tongue. Natasha impatiently grabbed them from her, rifling through the pages, counting ten of them.

"They're all here. I must get them back to Thanatos so we can complete the ritual tonight." She looked at Morgan and Jake. "I think you two will join us. We need a sacrifice and after the trouble you've caused, he will be pleased to have you as a gift to the Lord of Darkness."

CHAPTER 29

Sedlec, Kutna Hora, Czech Republic, 11.42pm

MORGAN AND JAKE WERE thrust out of the van into the blackness of the Czech night, their hands still cuffed with plastic ties. The drive from Karlsruhe east to the Czech Republic had taken only five hours on the fast German roads but they had been cramped and uncomfortable. The journey had passed in silence; any attempt at conversation had been met with a thud in the ribs from the weapons of the guards. When she realized where they were, Morgan knew they would have passed close to Nuremberg where Durer had lived and carved the images. She and Jake had been cuffed to a bench in the back of the van so she hadn't been able to see the route but now they had reached their destination, it all made sense.

"Sedlec," she said. "It's the bone church. The Devil's Bible once rested here and Arkady Novotsky's grave is here too."

A figure loomed out of the darkness.

"Indeed, my father rests just over there." Milan Noble stepped from the shadows, his chiseled features etched in the lamplight and he reached forward to trace Morgan's cheek. Natasha stepped in front of him, blocking his hand with her body, stopping any show of interest in her perceived rival.

"I have the pages. I thought these two might be good for

sacrifice."

She gave Milan the pages, and he held them to the light, his eyes skimming the words.

"These are a match to the Devil's Bible. Well done Natasha."

Milan pulled her to him and kissed her deeply, all thought of Morgan forgotten. Natasha moaned as he bit down on her lip, drawing blood.

"Get a room," Jake said and was rewarded with a thump in the gut by one of the guards.

Milan stood tall, his arm still around Natasha. Morgan noticed that his hand moved down to cup her belly in a protective manner. Was another secret hidden there?

"We will perform the ritual at midnight, for the words unleash power to those who speak them. Tomorrow they will be released to the world and our armageddon will truly begin."

"You don't have to do this Milan," Morgan pleaded. "You can still burn those pages. Leave Zoebios to do good in the world. It's your legacy."

Milan stood taller.

"In the shadow of my father's house you dare talk about legacy. I am finishing his work for life only finds its fulfillment in death and Thanatos is death in all its glory. The prophecy can be fulfilled by these words and the way I can send it to the world. A quarter of the world will die Morgan, but you won't live to see it happen."

He spun round and strode into the church. Natasha smiled with triumph and followed him while the guards forced Morgan and Jake forwards down the path and into the Sedlec church. They were joined by Armen Harghada, who smiled at Morgan, eyes hooded like a snake impassively waiting for the death of its prey so it can feed.

Inside, the macabre church was lit with candles placed in bony candlesticks. Ancient fingers stretched towards heaven as wax dripped down them, creating a form of pale flesh. The air was heavy with smoky incense, the scent cloying. Morgan breathed it in and felt her awareness blur, as if the smoke was carrying part of her away. The altar of human skeletons gleamed in the flickering light and on it the huge book, the Devil's Bible, lay open.

Milan carefully placed the missing pages onto it and ran his fingers over the parchment. Morgan could see he was already reading the words in his head and for a second, she remembered how it had felt when she had glanced them back in Germany. It had seemed like the first touch of a drug that you just wanted to sink into, but a pleasure that would devour if you would just say the words aloud. Part of her wanted to rip the pages from him and speak the words herself but she also saw in her mind the precipice that those words stood upon. She felt like she was clinging to a rock above a sea of molten fire that would destroy in bursts of flame. Those possessed by the drug of the words would fling themselves into the holocaust with no care for their coming destruction.

Milan raised his hands above his head in divine supplication. There was a silence in the crypt, as if angels and demons crouched in the bony arches held their breath, waiting for the decision of this one man to leap into darkness or reach towards the light.

Milan Noble began to read aloud from the Devil's Bible, speaking the curses that would empower him with the might of the Evil One. He felt the surge in his body as he spoke the ancient words, a humming through his veins as if he was possessed by a tremendous force. The image of Satan inscribed on the page filled his vision, plumes of sulfur rising from his body as he slashed through bloody chunks of flesh from the victim beneath him. Milan felt invincible. This was what his father had sought, this communion with the dark side, with the shadow. He hadn't truly believed it himself until this moment but now he was becoming something new. He could feel the change welling up inside.

His gut twisted, his heart raced. This was a freedom of spirit he hadn't expected and in that moment he saw the heavens open and the earth split with the fires of Hell beneath. He saw God turn his back and leave the demons to take what they now owned. Milan shouted the final word in glorious release and a flash of light burst into his brain, illuminating everything. Then he doubled over in pain, retching as if a serpent had unwound itself in the pit of his stomach. His muscles spasmed and he fell to the floor, twitching, head rolling, as the final words echoed through his brain.

Morgan watched in amazement as Milan fell to the ground in what looked like an epileptic fit. She saw ripples under his skin as if something was crawling under there, trying to get out and it looked like he was physically changing. Was it real, she thought, or just the effects of the heavy incense smoke? As Natasha, Harghada and the bodyguards rushed to help Milan, Morgan saw their chance to escape but Jake shook his head.

"We can't leave. We have to finish this," he whispered. Milan's retching had turned into grunting, an animal roar that reverberated in the bony chamber.

"Then we must at least get out of the way," Morgan replied. "We can get up to the balcony there and wait to see what happens."

Together they crept up the balcony stairs and looked down upon the scene unfolding below. The shimmering incense smoke partially obscured their view, like looking through opaque glass. Finally, Milan stopped twisting and lay still and as Natasha stepped away, Morgan caught a glimpse of his face. Milan's beauty seemed grotesquely enhanced, every angle of his chiseled face exaggerated into sharpness by a diabolical metamorphosis. He looked like a deadly angel, one of those that loved human women too much. As his eyes opened, Natasha backed away, running for the door.

One of the bodyguards bent down to help Milan but the man's head exploded as a bony spear thrust up through his jaw. Milan ripped the head from the man's shoulders in one swipe of his makeshift blade and then spun to his feet. In a swift motion, he smashed the other guard into the altar, then grabbed his head, dashing it repeatedly on the stone until it ran red with blood and mashed brains. The door slammed as Natasha left and Morgan heard the scraping of the lock, shutting them in here with the demon. Milan snarled and advanced on Harghada who was curled in the corner, whimpering.

"Here, you bastard, have a go at me."

Morgan heard Jake's voice in the nave. He had slipped back down and was trying to draw Milan away from the cowering Doctor. Damn him. Always playing the hero, Morgan thought. She could see Jake in the haze of smoke, brandishing a femur like a club in one hand and a length of chain in the other. He had smashed the femur so the broken end was sword-sharp, a bony spike that matched Milan's weapon. For a second, she saw how magnificent he was, a lean gladiator fighting the ancient battle against evil. In opposition, Milan was a sculpted Lucifer, ripples of energy pulsing down his long arms.

"You're not enough to beat me, Jake Timber. You and all here will die and I will take this curse to the world."

Milan snarled and spun towards the cowering Doctor, daring Jake to attack him. Jake whipped the chain under his legs to try and stop him reaching his prey. Milan leaped, an impossible animal bound that barreled him into his victim. He ripped and bit at the man's flesh as Harghada screamed in agony and terror. Jake rushed in to hammer Milan with the femur but with a powerful feral kick, he was sent flying backwards. The brutal blow smashed him head first into the stack of deconstructed skeletons which crashed to the floor around him. Jake lay there, unmoving.

Milan silenced Harghada's scream by slashing his face off with the bone blade. He seemed not at all hurried this time, hacking at his victim and biting until the once arrogant Doctor was just a bloody lump of flesh. Morgan watched the horror, frozen by fear. The carnage had happened in just a few seconds. She should run like Natasha; she could still get away, but she had to get to Jake. He had come back for her during Pentecost and she wouldn't leave him to this bloody end now. She saw Milan's eyes flick to Jake and knew she had to act.

"Up here," she called. "Don't think it's over yet."

"Morgan," he said, his voice a perverse caress. "You shall be the perfect sacrifice to my dark Lord. Will you come down or I shall come up there and get you?"

His voice was terrifying in its normality, a voice that had whispered sweet things in her ear, tempting her with promises. But the mouth that would have given her pleasure was now dripping with the blood of his victims. Morgan's rational mind was still questioning the reality of his transformation. Was the power of the Devil's Bible real? Or was this heady smoke creating hallucinations of horror? She hesitated.

"I'm coming up then," he said. "I'll finish your boyfriend afterwards for I think watching you die will be his torture."

Morgan crouched with her back to the balcony railing. She could hear Milan walking across the floor of the church and in seconds, he would be up here and on her. She looked around desperately. What could she use to defend herself?

In that moment, a calm descended on her and Elian's

voice came to her over the years. He had died in a battle for their lives just as this one and after the bullets had carved a path through his body, he had spoken in his dying breath *'Morgan, you must live for me.'* She owed it to him, the man she had loved so much and now Jake, the man she had begun to trust. She would not go down cowering in fear to this demon.

Jumping to her feet, she tried to calm her breath and still her mind. Focus on this moment alone, she thought. There's always an option. Then she saw the chandelier and knew it was her chance. She couldn't fight in this enclosed space with no weapon. She climbed onto the railing and looked down at Milan, his body drenched in gore. It looked like he was changing, becoming more demon and less man. He looked up and snarled, lips curling back over perfect teeth stained with blood. What was this curse, Morgan thought, that it could turn man into unhallowed beast so fast?

Milan began to climb, using the skeletal ornamentation to pull himself up towards the balcony. Morgan looked out towards the chandelier. She had one chance to make it or she would break her own body landing on the flagstones far below and then he would rip what was left of her apart. She could see Jake stirring in the pile of shattered bones but his eyes were still closed so she had to keep Milan focused on her.

Just as an obscenely muscled arm reached the top of the balcony, Morgan leapt into space, flinging herself towards the chandelier, praying its fragile arms would hold her weight. The macabre bone structure rattled as she grabbed for it, swinging away from the balcony, her face up against the humerus bones of hundreds of plague dead. Milan laughed at her stupidity and she realized that she would inevitably swing back towards him, but over the other side was another balcony. If she could swing to it in the next pass, she could climb down on that side before he reached her and grab a weapon.

As the chandelier swung back towards Milan, Morgan tucked her legs up, daring to hope that he wouldn't be able to reach her swinging body. The bark of his laugh pierced her thoughts and she felt the swipe of pain in her back and side as his blade connected, ripping open a deep wound. But she held on and swung back to the far balcony.

"First blood, Morgan," Milan rasped. "The rest I will spill on the altar as I take you to my Master."

As the chandelier reached its zenith, she jumped, using her legs as leverage. She didn't quite make it over the balcony railing but smashed into it, opening her wound further. She gasped, clutching with desperate hands as she began to slip back. Her fingers found the bony protuberances of another sculpture and she stopped falling, but she knew Milan would be on her soon enough. She scrabbled to try to climb over, but the cold fingers of pain were sneaking up from her side. But she wouldn't go down running from him. She needed a weapon and then she would face what he had become and send him to Hell.

Jake's head was fuzzy from the fall and the effects of the incense smoke but he was still alive. He heard the barking laugh and knew he had to stand. He pushed himself up onto his hands and knees, head spinning. He looked up to see Morgan hanging from the balcony opposite where they had been hiding and Milan about to jump after her. Jake saw the spiked femur on the ground and with a great surge of energy, grabbed it and ran towards them.

Milan jumped and his fingers grabbed the bony candelabra arms. The light swung but the man was too heavy and a crack resounded through the church as the fitting broke.

Jake leaped forward with the femur and held it like a

lance of faith towards heaven.

Milan fell, tangled in the thousand bone chandelier, and with a sickening scream he was impaled even as he crushed Jake beneath him.

Morgan watched in horror as Jake was buried beneath Milan's body and the twisted pile of bones. With renewed strength, she pulled herself over the balcony, hand clutched to her side, trying to stem the bleeding. Limping now, she stumbled down the stairs and out into the nave. The pile of bones and flesh hadn't moved.

"Jake, can you hear me?" she called in desperation, scrabbling to pull the bones off. Then she saw Milan, eyes glassy, his mouth open in shock, but his face was as beautiful as the day she had first met him. The demon inside him was gone and he was transformed back to man in death. The bony femur had lanced through his body and thrust out through his chest, ripping through bloody flesh. Morgan was crying now, tears running down her face in shock and horror and in anguish for Jake.

"Be alright, just be alright," she whispered, as she dragged Milan's body off the pile, uncaring of the dead. As she rolled it away, she found Jake underneath, his face pale but he was still breathing, a ragged, rasping sound.

"Jake, can you hear me? Jake?" Morgan felt the weak pulse at his neck. His body was bloody but looked more crushed than ripped open. Her own wound throbbed and she had to get help before she too passed out. Remembering the dead guards, Morgan crawled to the nearest one. His ragged face was mauled, his body lying in a pool of congealed blood. She rifled through his pocket, finding the cell phone. Dizzy now, she dialed the ARKANE emergency number and as the voice asked for identification, she slipped into unconsciousness.

CHAPTER 30

Private ward, John Radcliffe Hospital. Oxford, England. A week later.

MORGAN OPENED HER EYES, this time with clarity. She had felt the darkness ebbing and flowing, a comforting sleep of drugs and exhaustion that had kept her under. Her dreams had been a freak's gallery of bones, demons and the rotting face of a little girl, buried in splintered corpses, but now she felt ready to wake up.

The hospital room was small but tastefully furnished in moss green and sky blue and the window looked out onto the spired city of Oxford. She was home. There were flowers on the table and cards, including a hand-drawn one with a little girl holding roses on it. At least that's what it looked like. Morgan smiled at the thought of her niece coloring carefully for her Auntie and she felt a pang of need to see her family.

"Good, you're awake." The staff nurse bustled in, smiled at her and checked the monitors. "There've been lots of visitors. You're a popular lady. How are you feeling?"

"Like I've been run over several times," Morgan whispered.

"I'll bring you some tea." The nurse turned to go.

"Please wait," Morgan said. "What happened to my partner, Jake Timber. He would have been brought in at the same time as me?"

The nurse looked concerned.

"I'll try to find out. In the meantime, you need to rest."

Morgan tried to sit up, but a bolt of agony flashed up her side and she fell back on the bed. Her fingers explored the bandaged wound where she had been slashed. It had been deep but must have missed anything vital, as she was still here. She found the buttons for the bed control and eased it into a sitting position.

"Shall I come back later?" Marietti stood in the doorway, a takeaway coffee steaming in his hand from The Missing Bean, her favorite coffee shop. He held it towards her. "Or can I tempt you with this?"

"You're a saint, Director." Morgan took the cup and raised it for a tentative sip, the hot coffee a balm to her parched throat and the caffeine a welcome kick to her soul. Everyone is allowed one addiction, she thought. "Now, where's Jake?"

Marietti looked grave.

"He's been in and out of surgery. The kidney issues caused by crush syndrome and shock have been the most severe but he's now stabilized in Intensive Care. He wouldn't have made it without your call which enabled the swift extraction by the local team."

Morgan took another sip of coffee and looked out of the window towards the fields of north Oxford. Tears pricked her eyes with concern but also relief. Jake would pull through, he was a strong man, but she needed some answers about what happened.

"What did you find at the church? Did you take Milan's body?"

"I know what you must have seen Morgan. I saw photos of the carnage left behind. Something ripped those men apart, but there's no evidence other than the injuries."

Morgan shook her head.

"There must be evidence. Did you test the body? He looked so normal at the end, but Director, I swear, he was turning into a demonic creature after speaking the words from the Devil's Bible." She faltered. "But then there was a haze of hallucinogenic smoke in the church. Perhaps what I saw was the effect of the drugs?"

Morgan rubbed her eyes, trying to clear her head. It was hard to believe what she remembered and there was no rational explanation. Marietti put his hand on her arm.

"This is what we do, Morgan. This is ARKANE. We take these secrets and we bury them. We keep people safe in their snug faith. The Devil's Bible is buried deep in the vaults now with the missing pages intact. It's in a box, embedded in concrete and the location has been plastered over. No one will find it again. Milan's body was patched up as best we could and a sympathetic coroner in the Czech government helped with the press release about his death. Officially, he committed suicide at his Czech home because of the scandal of the Zoebios eugenics program."

Morgan sighed.

"I didn't take the threat of Thanatos or the Devil's Bible seriously before, and I don't know what to believe now."

"We're all flawed Morgan and we all have our own demons." Marietti met her eyes, the violet slash bright. "I know you have your doubts about me and Ben has told you of old enemies and generations of lies. But whatever the mistakes of the past, we keep trying. There is real evil in this world and the line between the physical and spiritual wavers. The gap between is where ARKANE must work. If you stay with us, you will see many more things that will make you question what you believe."

"Of course I want to stay." She said, with no hesitation. "My own questions can only be explored by these experiences and I can protect my family better if I'm involved."

Marietti nodded. "That's good, because I need you back as soon as you can get out this bed."

"Why, what's happened?"

"There's been a ritual murder at the Museum of Egyptian Antiquities in Cairo," Marietti replied. "A number of exhibits have been ransacked but it's certain that select pieces from the Amarna period are missing."

"That's the time of Pharaoh Akhenaten, when Egypt moved briefly into monotheism." Morgan said, her eyes brightening with interest. "It's thought by some that Moses was a priest in that time and that the Exodus happened shortly after."

Marietti looked serious.

"From the security cameras, it looks like Natasha El-Behery is behind this. The local ARKANE team is certain that she's searching for the Ark of the Covenant. I know you'll want to be part of the team, but are you well enough?"

Morgan's eyes were cobalt steel.

"Director, I'll do anything to get my hands on Natasha. After what she's done, you have to let me go. I can start the research right now."

"The doctors will have to clear you but I'll have Martin send over the information for you to look at. Now, let's see if we can get you in to see Jake."

He helped her out of bed, waving away the frantic nurse who tried to stop them. Morgan stifled a groan and forced herself to move through the pain and into the wheelchair. Grabbing the portable IV, Marietti wheeled her out of the room and down the corridor to Intensive Care where Jake had a private room with a glass door. Morgan stretched forward and placed her hand palm inward on the glass. Be well, my friend, she thought. But as she looked at him, body lying like a corpse on the hospital bed, oxygen mask on his face, tubes in and out of his body, Morgan knew she would be going to Egypt without her partner.

* * *

Morgan and Jake's adventures continue in
Ark of Blood, available now.

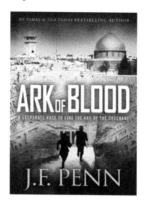

*One woman's desperate race to find the
Ark of the Covenant - and save the world
from a devastating Holy War.*

Cairo, Egypt. When the curator of the Museum of Antiquities is slaughtered in a horrific ritual by a group wearing the masks of Ancient Egyptian deities, local authorities ask for help from ARKANE, the agency tasked with investigating religious and paranormal events.

In Washington DC, a decapitated Arab body is discovered. The head is placed on the replica Ark of the Covenant along with a chilling message that warns of a terrifying escalation of violence in the Middle East.

ARKANE agent, British-Israeli psychologist Dr Morgan Sierra, must race against time to uncover the real Ark - aware that her nemesis, the vicious mercenary Natasha, is also in the hunt and out for bloody revenge. Morgan travels across Egypt and Jordan, retracing the steps of the Biblical Exodus and following a trail of clues that takes her into the mists of history - and mortal danger...

ENJOYED CRYPT OF BONE?

If you loved the book and have a moment to spare, I would really appreciate a short review on the page where you bought the book. Your help in spreading the word is gratefully appreciated and reviews make a huge difference to helping new readers find the series. Thank you!

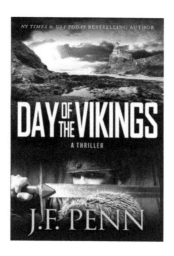

Get a free copy of the bestselling thriller, *Day of the Vikings*, ARKANE book 5, when you sign up to join my Reader's Group. You'll also be notified of new releases, giveaways and receive personal updates from behind the scenes of my thrillers.

WWW.JFPENN.COM/FREE

* * *

Day of the Vikings, an ARKANE thriller

A ritual murder on a remote island under the shifting skies of the aurora borealis.

A staff of power that can summon Ragnarok, the Viking apocalypse.

When Neo-Viking terrorists invade the British Museum in London to reclaim the staff of Skara Brae, ARKANE agent Dr. Morgan Sierra is trapped in the building along with hostages under mortal threat.

As the slaughter begins, Morgan works alongside psychic Blake Daniel to discern the past of the staff, dating back to islands invaded by the Vikings generations ago.

Can Morgan and Blake uncover the truth before Ragnarok is unleashed, consuming all in its wake?

Day of the Vikings is a fast-paced, supernatural thriller set in London and the islands of Orkney, Lindisfarne and Iona. Set in the present day, it resonates with the history and myth of the Vikings.

If you love an action-packed thriller,
you can get Day of the Vikings for free now:

WWW.JFPENN.COM/FREE

Day of the Vikings features Dr. Morgan Sierra from the ARKANE thrillers, and Blake Daniel from the London Crime Thrillers, but it is also a stand-alone novella that can be read and enjoyed separately.

AUTHOR'S NOTE

I LOVE TO MELD the real and the possible in my writing, ideally so you don't even know which is which. Research is also one of the most fun parts of being an author. Here are some of the aspects woven into the book that you might be interested to know more about and as ever, any mistakes are my own.

Obedience to authority research

"When you think of the long and gloomy history of man, you will find far more hideous crimes have been committed in the name of obedience than have been committed in the name of rebellion."

CP Snow, "Either-Or" (1961)

This topic has fascinated me since I first read of Stanley Milgram's experiments based on demonstrating that the Nazi atrocities would have been perpetrated by any of us given the same situation. The Stanford prison experiment took this further and I urge you to read Philip Zimbardo's 'The Lucifer Effect: How Good People Turn Evil' if you're interested in more detail. The assassination of Israeli Prime Minister Yitzhak Rabin in 1995 was also a turning point in my own life. I had been studying Arabic with the intention of working in the Middle East. The fact that Rabin was killed by an extremist Jew dashed my own hopes of working for peace in the troubled country to which I am so emotionally attached. It seemed there were just too many obstacles to a real solution. The killer's words, "God told me to do it" remained with me and were part of the inspiration for this book. After switching to study Theology at the University of Oxford, I specialized in the psychology of religion. I wrote my thesis on fundamentalism and why people commit violence in the name of God. Abraham's agreement to sacrifice his son Isaac was one of my influences and is also examined in Soren Kierkegaard's 'Fear and Trembling'.

I have written more extensively on this at: www.joannapenn.com/obedience/

The God Helmet

Dr Michael Persinger, speaking about the God Helmet on a UK BBC Horizon documentary

"The fundamental experience is the sensed presence, and our data indicate that the sensed presence, the feeling of another entity of something beyond yourself, perhaps bigger than yourself … can be stimulated by simply activating the right hemisphere, particularly the temporal lobe."

Michael Persinger is a cognitive neuroscience researcher and the God Helmet is one of his inventions. His research was inspired by temporal lobe epilepsy and the visions of

God and the supernatural that can occur to people in that state. His research received so much media attention that even atheist Richard Dawkins tried it. He didn't report anything significant, but many others who have tried the helmet have had unusual experiences. Of course the smaller version that Zoebios created is my own invention but I would love to give this technology a try.

You can read more at: www.joannapenn.com/god-helmet/

The Devil's Bible

The Codas Gigas is indeed the largest medieval manuscript in the world. It was at Sedlec for a period of time and is now kept in Sweden. It's called the Devil's Bible because of the rather comical illustrations of the Devil in the book and there really are 10 missing pages.

You can watch a documentary on it here: www.joannapenn. com/devils-bible/

Art and architecture

The ossuaries and catacombs featured in the book are all real places. You can visit the Paris catacombs, Sedlec, Evora and Palermo and see the macabre arrangement of bones. Once I had discovered Sedlec I knew I had my final scene and it was synchronicity that the Devil's Bible had been held there by the monks. The apocalyptic woodcuts of Albrecht Durer are real, as are the details about his life. It's feasible to think he would have seen the Devil's Bible, although the woodblocks haven't actually been split open to see if they contain the missing pages. Or have they?

The painting in Marietti's office by Dali is one of my own favorites and the images Morgan examines in the ARKANE database are all real paintings. William Blake and John Martin are renowned for their Biblical scenes. The Treasures of Heaven exhibition at the British Museum inspired the scene on religious relics.

MORE BOOKS BY J.F. PENN

Thanks for joining Morgan, Jake and the
ARKANE team. The adventures continue …

Stone of Fire #1
Crypt of Bone #2
Ark of Blood #3
One Day in Budapest #4
Day of the Vikings #5
Gates of Hell #6
One Day in New York #7
Destroyer of Worlds #8
End of Days #9
Valley of Dry Bones #10

If you like **crime thrillers with an edge of the supernatural**,
join Detective Jamie Brooke and museum researcher Blake
Daniel, in the London Crime Thriller trilogy:

Desecration #1
Delirium #2
Deviance #3

If you enjoy **dark fantasy,** check out:

Map of Shadows, Mapwalkers #1
Risen Gods
American Demon Hunters: Sacrifice

A Thousand Fiendish Angels:
Short stories based on Dante's Inferno

The Dark Queen

More books coming soon.

You can sign up to be notified of new releases, giveaways
and pre-release specials - plus, get a free book!

WWW.JFPENN.COM/FREE

ABOUT J.F.PENN

J.F.Penn is the Award-nominated, New York Times and USA Today bestselling author of the ARKANE supernatural thrillers, London Crime Thrillers, and the Mapwalker dark fantasy series, as well as other standalone stories.

Her books weave together ancient artifacts, relics of power, international locations and adventure with an edge of the supernatural. Joanna lives in Bath, England and enjoys a nice G&T.

* * *

You can sign up for a free thriller,
Day of the Vikings, and updates from behind the scenes,
research, and giveaways at:

WWW.JFPENN.COM/FREE

* * *

Connect at:
www.JFPenn.com
joanna@JFPenn.com
www.Facebook.com/JFPennAuthor
www.Instagram.com/JFPennAuthor
www.Twitter.com/JFPennWriter

* * *

For writers:

Joanna's site, www.TheCreativePenn.com, helps people write, publish and market their books through articles, audio, video and online courses.

She writes non-fiction for authors under Joanna Penn and has an award-nominated podcast for writers, The Creative Penn Podcast.

ACKNOWLEDGEMENTS

As always, my love and thanks to Jonathan. You're the stability from which I can experiment with this new writing life.

Thanks to my editor and official first reader, Jacqueline Penn, who did an incredibly detailed job on editing and who continues to bring a fresh perspective to my writing. Thanks for keeping me honest, Mum!

A huge thank you to my beta-readers: my husband Jonathan; my friend and mentor Orna Ross www.OrnaRoss. com who brought a much needed professional slant; action-adventure author David Wood www.davidwoodonline. blogspot.com/ who brings a kick-ass perspective; and to Arthur Penn, my Dad, who is also an art history special-ist and writer himself. I couldn't have done it without you guys.

Thanks to my cover designer, the lovely Derek Murphy who did a brilliant job: www.bookcovers.creativindie.com/ Thanks also to Liz Broomfield from www.libroediting.com/ who did the final copyedit on the last draft over the Christ-mas period as I just had to get the book out in 2011. Thanks to Jane at www.jdsmith-design.com/ who did the interior for the print edition.

Thank you to my fantastic tribe at The Creative Penn and also my writing and blogging friends on Twitter @thecreativepenn. In the last 3 years I've found my niche online and it has changed my life beyond imagining. Thank you for being part of the journey.

A final thanks to my friends from Rio in Australia who supported me through the beginning stages of being an author. To Heidi and Damian, Lizette, Hervais, Ian, Michael, Derek, Bruce and all the boys on the PTP team. I miss you guys, but this is the life for me!